W9-BNR-178

DI'S HALLOWEEN PARTY—
DI, TRIX, HONEY

BRIAN'S
JET-PROPELLED
BUGGY!

Bobby and friend

Bob-Whites of the Glen

THE CHAMP

SITZMARK JIM!

Trixie Belden #8

The Black Jacket Mystery

by Kathryn Kenny
illustrated by Paul Frame
cover illustration by Michael Koelsch

Random House 🏠 New York

www.randomhouse.com/kids

Library of Congress Cataloging-in-Publication Data
Kenny, Kathryn.
[Trixie Belden and the black jacket mystery]
The black jacket mystery / by Kathryn Kenny ; illustrated by Paul Frame ; cover illustration by Michael Koelsch. — 1st Random House ed.
    p. cm. — (Trixie Belden ; #8)
Originally published: Trixie Belden and the black jacket mystery. New York : Whitman Books, 1961.
SUMMARY: While organizing an ice carnival to raise funds for her pen pal's school library, Trixie investigates a mysterious problem facing Regan and a run of thefts and accidents in the neighborhood.
ISBN 0-375-82979-2 (trade) — ISBN 0-375-92979-7 (lib. bdg.)
[1. Mystery and detective stories. 2. Carnivals—Fiction. 3. Stealing—Fiction.]
I. Frame, Paul, ill. II. Koelsch, Michael. III. Title. IV. Series.

PZ7.K396Bl 2004 [Fic]—dc22 2003025040

Printed in the United States of America 10 9 8 7 6 5 4 3 2 1

First Random House Edition
RANDOM HOUSE and colophon are registered trademarks of Random House, Inc.

CONTENTS

Chapter 1
An Emergency

"Bobby! If you don't hold still, I'll never have you ready in time to catch your bus!" Trixie was trying her best to get her six-year-old brother into his winter overcoat.

But Bobby had broken away again, and with his coat dangling from one arm, had plunged under the dresser in search of his missing crayons. His voice came out muffled. "Gotta take my crayons this morning. Miss Elephant says so!"

"Oh, dear!" Thirteen-year-old Trixie ran her hands despairingly through her unruly mop of sandy curls. "I keep trying to tell you her name's Miss Elliman, and you better call her that. Elli-*m-a-n*. Not Ele-*phant!*" she scolded. "And hurry up!"

"Got 'um!" Bobby wriggled out from under the dresser clutching a handful of crayons and a crumpled box. "Zip me!"

Trixie hustled him into the overcoat and zippered it hastily. "Now sit down just half a minute, and I'll be ready!"

She knew it would be a long half minute, but there were certain rules in the Belden household about tidying up bedrooms before leaving for school, and she had no choice. She whipped the covers off her bed and started to remake it.

"Make tracks, small squaw, or you'll miss the bus!" It was Mart, poking his head in at the door. Mart was eleven months older than Trixie and was often mistaken for her twin. They had the same sturdy build and blond hair, but Mart kept his in a short crew cut to avoid the curls that made the "twin" appearance stronger. Lately he had grown a couple of inches taller than Trixie and was extremely proud of it, except that he was growing out of his clothing.

"Oh, Mart, could you—just this once—take Bobby to the bus?" Trixie appealed.

"Seems to me you get paid to do that," Mart teased. "Not a chance, sister dear!"

Trixie swallowed hard and turned back to the bed-making feeling very sorry for herself. She didn't see Mart crook his finger mysteriously at Bobby, or Bobby get up hastily and tiptoe to the door to join his big brother and disappear down the hall with him.

Trixie smoothed the covers and folded her quilt. "There! I won't be another minute!" she flung over her shoulder toward the spot where Bobby had been sitting. Then she stopped short. He was gone.

Trixie ran to the window and looked out. Mart, with Bobby firmly by the hand, was going out the front gate into Glen Road. He *had* been teasing her, as usual.

"You're late, dear. What's wrong with you this morning?" Her mother came into the room.

Trixie sighed and started to brush her unruly curls into a semblance of neatness. "I overslept. I was awake 'most all night, thinking about Dolores and Lupe and the earthquake, wondering what the B.W.G.'s could do to help."

Dolores and Lupe Perez were pen pals of Trixie's and of her best friend, Honey Wheeler. Their letters, received yesterday, had told of an earthquake that had partially destroyed their small village of San Isidro, located in a Mexican coast state.

The biggest tragedy to the Mexican girls had been the destruction of their school library. The B.W.G.'s, a secret club that Trixie and Honey had organized with their brothers a few months before, had gathered a lot of old schoolbooks for the small library and had found the Mexican girls delighted with the gift. They had written many times since, enthusiastically, about how much the books had helped them understand their northern neighbors.

"We've got to find more books for them," Trixie told her mother.

"You will, dear. I'm sure of it." Mrs. Belden smiled. She knew that Trixie was always full of ideas. Some of the ideas might plunge Trixie and her brothers and friends into all sorts of complications, but somehow they always came out of them safely. Usually, it was due to Trixie's "detectiving," with the assistance of Honey Wheeler, her closest friend.

A few minutes later, Trixie sped down the long path in front of the neat little farmhouse and through the front gate of the white picket fence. She was well bundled up against the late February chill of the small but lovely valley on the east shore of the great Hudson River. It had snowed a couple of days before, but the road to Sleepyside Junior-Senior High School was always the first to be cleared. Which meant, alas, that the Beldens and their next-door neighbors, Honey and her adopted brother Jim, had few days off from school because of snow-blocked roads.

Honey and Jim were waiting with Mart at the bus stop as Trixie staggered up, breathless.

The high school bus was just coming around the corner into Glen Road and Bobby's grade school bus had already left with Bobby safely aboard.

"Whew! I made it!" Trixie announced between gasps. She knew better than to thank Mart in front of their friends for taking Bobby to the bus for her. Mart would have been embarrassed. He always tried to "play it cool," as he called it. She decided to save her thanks till they were alone.

Honey was taller and slimmer than Trixie, although they were practically the same age. Her shoulder-length light-brown hair and her soft hazel eyes had brought her the nickname of Honey. Everyone used it, because it fitted her so well.

Honey's father was a millionaire. Their Manor House estate, that touched the borders of the Beldens' small Crabapple Farm, was a huge one. It had stood empty for several years before the Wheelers had bought it and moved in last summer. Mr. Wheeler had had the underbrush cleared off, a private game preserve established for hunting, and the mansion itself redecorated. His stables, in the charge of Bill Regan as head groom, held the finest of saddle horses.

Honey, an only child, had been lonely till they moved into the Manor House. Her parents were often away from home and she had been practically brought up by servants.

But after she and Trixie had met and become

friends at once, all had changed. They had had several exciting adventures together, during one of which they had helped Jim Frayne escape a cruel stepfather. Now adopted by the Wheelers, fifteen-year-old Jim was everything that Honey had dreamed a big brother could be.

Trixie's two older brothers and Jim Frayne were all members of the Bob-Whites of the Glen, the secret club that the girls had thought up last fall.

"Did you manage to think of any way the B.W.G.'s can find more books for the San Isidro school?" Honey asked as the bus drew up and stopped for them.

"Sort of," Trixie admitted. "But it's still only a glimmer. It could be fabulous if we can work it out!"

"Here she goes again, straight into orbit!" Mart sang out, and groaned loudly.

Jim chuckled. "It's been much too quiet since the antique sale excitement died down. I felt we were due for a launching soon!"

"Let's sit by ourselves," Trixie whispered hastily, and led the way to the empty rear of the bus. The B.W.G.'s always had their choice of seats because most of the other pupils of Sleepyside Junior-Senior High School lived closer to town than they did.

Mart promptly followed his sister and Honey up the aisle and Jim went along with a mischievous smile.

They plumped down in the seat ahead of the two girls, so they wouldn't miss a word.

Trixie shielded her mouth with her hand as she leaned close to Honey. "I thought maybe we could have an ice carnival on your lake at the end of this month. You know, before the ice starts to melt," she whispered. "A benefit show!"

"Marvelous!" Honey whispered. "Go on!"

Trixie was so excited as the thoughts started racing through her brain that she forgot to whisper, and her voice rose sharply, "We'll have games and skating races and we'll give away prizes—"

Mart's voice came from the seat ahead. "Our esteemed treasurer will love the part about prizes," it said loudly, "considering the irrefutable fact that the club treasury is now practically empty. Madame President seems to have taken no cognizance of the fact." Mart liked to try to puzzle Trixie by using big words of which she wouldn't know the meanings. Usually, he succeeded, but this time Trixie only gave a disdainful but unladylike snort and resumed her whispered conversation with Honey.

Brian, their sixteen-year-old brother, was club treasurer. He was a senior at Sleepyside, having skipped a grade, and was getting ready to go to college next year to start studying to become a doctor. Brian was tall like his father and had the same dark good looks. Between his schoolwork and the chores he did, both at home and helping with the Wheeler horses, he was always busy. His day started early and ended late, but he always kept some time for the Bob-Whites along the way.

"Have you tried out your latest brainstorm on our big brother?" Mart interrupted the whispering to ask.

"I haven't seen Brian today, but I'm sure he'll think of something helpful," Trixie told him coolly. "He always does." She paused pointedly and then added sweetly, "Why, even *you* two might come up with an idea if you strained your tiny brains a little!"

"Ouch! She hit me!" Mart pretended to hold his head. "Unfair blow!"

"Silly character!" Trixie sniffed and went back to whispering to Honey.

The bus stopped just then to take on a crowd of their friends so the laughter and chatter and greetings put an end to any hope Mart had of thinking up a sharp answer. And any further talk about Trixie's brand-new carnival plans had to be postponed.

But all the rest of the day, whenever Trixie and Honey met briefly in the locker room or the corridors on their way to classes, they had exchanged quick excited whispers. "Tickets—posters to be made, prizes—where are we going to get them?" Trixie would ask. "What else are we forgetting? What are we going to need first?"

"Muscles for building the booths," Honey would giggle. "That means Jim and Mart. And Brian to drive his jalopy around Sleepyside handing out our posters *after* Jim finishes lettering them—and, oh, jillions of things!"

So it went till they were on the bus hurrying home to try out the idea on their parents. Both of them knew it would mean a lot of hard work to get the ice carnival put on, but they felt up to it. All the Bob-Whites had regular chores for which their parents paid them a few dollars a week, and if it wouldn't mean neglecting those chores, or half-doing them, they were sure their parents wouldn't object. Besides, it was for a good cause.

Trixie watched her friend hurry up along the wide driveway to the Manor House. In the late winter afternoon sunshine, her home looked as cold as an ice palace, sitting among its snow-covered lawns. *I'm glad our house isn't on a hill,* Trixie thought. *Ours is lots smaller but it's lots "homier."* And she added with a contented smile, *We can always count on Moms being there to say hello.*

That last was something Honey couldn't always

depend on, Trixie knew. Her father's business connections made it necessary for her mother to be very social. And lots of times they had to rush off to Washington or some other place at a moment's notice. When they did, there was only Miss Trask to be "family." She was a very kindly person, the house supervisor, and fond of Honey. But she couldn't take the place of Honey's real folks.

"Guess we Beldens are lucky not to be rich!" Trixie chuckled to herself as she started away up the road toward her own small home.

There would be warmth in the sunny Belden kitchen, and Moms would be bustling about starting dinner. Dad would soon be home from his job at the bank in Sleepyside, and he liked to smell meat roasting and cake baking.

Moms would be wearing one of his own mother's big, old-fashioned, starched, white aprons while she worked. Not that she ever slopped anything on herself, but because Dad's mother and grandmother had worn them in that very same kitchen. There had been Beldens at Crabapple Farm for six generations, and there was even a rumor that Washington Irving had boarded with them while he was writing "Rip Van Winkle." *And they all wore aprons,* she thought grimly. *Glad I don't have to*

marry a Belden. My house is going to be run by push buttons. I may not even have a kitchen!

With that hopeful thought, she went around to the kitchen door to scrape the mud off her saddle shoes. As she came in sight of the rear door, she was astonished to recognize Starlight, one of the Wheeler horses, tied close by. Somebody from the Wheelers' must be visiting, but who?

The window of the service porch was open a few inches, and a big, masculine voice that she knew at once boomed out. "I wouldn't have bothered you with it, Mrs. Belden," Regan, the Wheelers' head groom, was saying, "but Miss Trask said you or Mr. Belden might have some idea what I can do. It's got me beside myself, worrying."

Trixie had never heard big, red-haired Regan speak in just that tone before. He never seemed to worry about anything except when she or the boys or Honey had been running the horses too much or had forgotten to clean the tack after a ride. And in those cases, he got just plain mad, and let them know it at once. Most of the time, though, he was good-natured and easygoing, and he and Tom, the chauffeur, had lots of jokes together.

Trixie felt sure that the trouble, whatever it was, had nothing to do with the horses her brothers and Jim had exercised this morning as usual. Regan would have had a ready answer for anything concerning them.

He was speaking again. "It's something I'm hoping to keep from any of the youngsters. There's no telling how they'd feel about it if they suspected the truth."

Trixie gasped out loud, and then clapped her hand over her mouth. This was getting worse every minute. She had no right to stand here and listen to anything that sounded as serious as this.

It took a lot of will power to stifle her curiosity and turn away, but she did it. She hurried around the house to the front door.

She took pains to close the front door loudly as she went in, and she sang a little as she strode along the hallway toward the kitchen. She hoped they would hear her.

Regan was still there, but there was a smile on his ruddy face as he stood at the rear door, cap in hand.

Trixie was just in time to hear his parting words.

"It sounds like the best idea, Mrs. Belden, and thanks a lot. If it doesn't work out, I don't know what more I can do. It could turn out good if I'm lucky, or just make things more mixed up."

Mrs. Belden nodded soberly. "It's worth trying. Good luck on it anyhow, Regan. I only wish we could do more to help."

Regan put on his cap, gave Trixie a nod and a brief smile, and with a quick "Good-by now," went out.

"What's bothering *him?*" Trixie tried to make her curiosity sound casual as she helped herself to a stalk of celery and munched on it.

"Something that doesn't concern you," her mother told her lightly, but Trixie heard her add under her breath as she turned away, "thank goodness!"

It was all very mysterious. And Trixie loved mysteries. Her mind kept flitting back to Regan and his "troubles" all the time that she was telling her mother the plans that were shaping up for the book benefit. It wasn't just idle curiosity. All the Beldens and their friends liked the broad-shouldered groom a lot, and if Trixie could find out what was bothering him, it was possible that they could do something to help him.

How could she learn what it was without asking questions? She couldn't ask her mother again. But there must be some way, and Trixie meant to find it!

Chapter 2
Mysterious Errand

"I think I'll phone Honey and just tell her that it's okay with you if we start working on our carnival plans right away," Trixie said suddenly, setting aside the bowl of potatoes she was about to peel.

Mrs. Belden sighed. "You have all evening to do that. Right now I hear Bobby running around up in your room. He's had a long nap since he came from school, and you know how fast he can turn your room into a wreck once he starts romping!"

"Gleeps! I'd better get him dressed and out of there!"

As Trixie hurried up the stairs, she could hear the kitchen extension ringing. She was tempted to come back to see if Honey was calling to report what her dad had said about the carnival plans, but a crash from her bedroom quickly changed her mind. She dashed there to see what mischief Bobby had gotten into this time.

"Oh, Bobby! My china cat!" The antique figure of a spotted, green-eyed cat was smashed into a hundred small pieces that were scattered over the floor around an overturned chair. Small Bobby was still sprawled on his hands and knees in the wreckage, where the chair had landed him.

His blue eyes stared up at her with a frightened expression and the tears started to roll down his fat cheeks. "I hurted myself!" he wailed.

"Oh, darling! Let me see!" The broken antique was forgotten as Trixie dropped to her knees and helped Bobby up out of the scattered fragments of the ornament. She made a quick examination of knees and elbows, but could find no cuts or bruises. "Thank goodness, you're all right!"

Bobby sniffed. "That ol' chair!" He kicked at the offending piece of furniture. "It wiggled, and I falled!"

Trixie looked at the remains of her antique cat and sighed. The head was almost in one piece except for one missing ear; but the body was beyond salvaging.

Bobby saw her expression and threw his arms around her neck. "I'm sorry. I only meant to pet Spotty. I'll buy you another one just like him if you won't cry."

Trixie hugged him hard and laughed. "Never mind, hon. I was sort of tired of dusting him, anyhow. And he was awfully old. You can't buy such funny-looking kitties nowadays."

Bobby sniffed doubtfully and then brightened.

"I'll give you my Teddy bear if you'd like." He said it bravely but Trixie knew he hoped she would say No.

"Goodness, no!" she said brightly. "He wouldn't be happy at all with me! He's always slept with you, and just think how he'd feel if I rolled on him some night and squashed him!"

"Yeah!" Bobby nodded vigorously. "Okay, then. I'll keep him myself, an' I'll find another kitty for you somewheres." He looked determined.

"Good! Maybe we'll find a live one some of these days, that looks just like Spotty, and Moms will let us keep him. How would that be?" she smiled. "A live one?"

Bobby nodded solemnly. "Without claws." And having settled that, he demanded, "How soon is supper?"

"Jeepers! I forgot. Moms said for us to hustle out to the kale patch and dig up some greens for Dad's supper. He's been talking about wanting some for the last three days and she wants to surprise him tonight!"

She hurried Bobby into his outdoor clothes and as he ran down to put his overshoes on in the front hall, she swept up the remains of Spotty. Dad's sister, Aunt Alicia, would have a fit when she found out that Spotty was among the missing. It was a family antique that she had sent Moms and Dad as a wedding present years ago.

The vegetable garden was still blanketed with the

two-day-old snow, but underneath, the kale was good as ever. They gathered a small basketful and then threw snowballs at each other and romped till they were both red-cheeked.

When they came into the warm kitchen, they were still laughing and rosy. "Here, Moms! We got 'um all. Now we won't have to eat that stuff any more till next year, will we?" Bobby asked hopefully.

Moms glanced at the store of vegetables in the basket. Then she said, keeping a straight face, "No, dear. We can start on the canned spinach instead."

Bobby's look of distress made them both laugh. "Better wash your hands and face now, son," his mother told him quickly. "We're having a very special guest to dinner and to spend the weekend with us."

Bobby was delighted to obey. He didn't care who the company was, just so it was company. And he dashed out to get ready without even asking.

"Who is it, Moms?" Trixie asked at once.

Moms laughed as she told her, "One of Bobby's special friends. A young lady who doesn't mind reading him his favorite stories over and over, even if they bore her!"

"Moms!" Trixie was delighted. "*Honey's* coming to stay here! Golly! What happened? What did she say?"

"Miss Trask phoned just now to see if it would be all right for Honey to spend the weekend with you. Her dad had an unexpected business conference called on the Coast and he and Mrs. Wheeler must leave tonight. And Jim had already arranged to be gone on a field trip with his biology group to study the Catskill wildlife. Honey would have been alone. Naturally, I said we'd love to have her!"

"Super!" Trixie hugged herself with delight. Then she had a disquieting thought. "Did Miss Trask say if Honey got a chance to ask them about the ice carnival?"

"No, dear. You'll find out as soon as Honey gets here."

"Maybe I ought to phone and tell her how glad I am she's coming?" Trixie couldn't wait.

"I don't think you need to, dear. But unless I get a little help, we're going to have a very late dinner, and I'm sure Dad won't like that."

"Gosh, I'm sorry, Moms!" Trixie flung off her heavy jacket and scarf. "I've been in such a dither all day."

"A perfectly understandable condition," Mart's voice said drily from the doorway, "brought on by a complete lack of mental co-ordination."

Moms held back a smile as Trixie faced her almost-twin with a stormy glare. She was used to their duels.

But this time, Trixie didn't merely sniff at her teasing brother, as usual. Instead, the glare faded into a cool stare as she said very deliberately, "The use of too many polysyllabic words is definitely a symptom of immaturity." Brian had spent half an hour at lunch time drilling her in that answer in preparation for just such a moment. She wasn't entirely sure what all the words meant, but Brian had assured her it would stop Mart in his tracks if she didn't bungle it.

It certainly had that effect. Mart's jaw dropped and he stared at his sister with a bewildered expression. Then as a delighted grin lit up her face, he turned and stalked down the hall without even trying to answer.

"Oh, boy! I've got to tell Brian! That really killed him!" Trixie chortled as she went to work on the potatoes.

Dinner was almost ready and Dad was home from Sleepyside and in his slippers when Honey came up the path carrying her overnight bag.

Trixie, clearing out a drawer in her dresser for Honey's things, glanced out of the window and saw her friend coming. She flung up the window to yell a welcome to her, but as she did, and with the words, "I'll be right down!" still unspoken on her lips, she stared in silent surprise.

Brian, looking dark and handsome as usual, and

24

wearing his new cashmere sweater and best trousers, was hurrying down the path to meet Honey.

Close at his heels, also slicked up and wearing his snazziest ski sweater, went Mart. Even at this distance Trixie could see that he was trying to overtake his longer-legged brother and be the one to help Honey carry her bag.

Brian won. He took the bag and got a sweet smile as his reward as he and Honey started up the path together.

But Mart wasn't left out. He promptly took his place on Honey's other side, and Trixie giggled as she saw him take over the conversation and Brian walk along silently.

"Hi, Honey! What's the verdict?" Trixie couldn't hold back the yell. She just had to know.

"Okay!" Honey called up to her. "Anything we want to do is all right with Dad!"

"Keen!" Trixie answered and closed the window. She watched through the pane a moment longer and saw that the rivalry for Honey's attention had started again after her interruption. She wore a satisfied smile as she finished clearing the drawer and started downstairs to bring up her guest. "Something tells me we've got a couple of willing workers lined up for the carnival!"

A few minutes later, she perched on the edge of the bed and watched Honey put her things away. "Thank goodness tomorrow's Saturday! Let's call a conference at the clubhouse in the morning after the boys have helped Regan with the horses. I can hardly wait to start on the carnival."

"They may be too busy. Miss Trask says Tom has to drive Regan to the city very early, and that means the boys will have all the responsibility of the stable, till they get back late Sunday night," Honey explained.

Trixie frowned. "I thought Miss Trask never let Regan and the chauffeur have the same day off. She's usually so fussy about wanting a man on the property, especially when your Dad's away. And Jim's gone now, too."

"It is sort of odd, isn't it? But she said it was an emergency of some kind."

"Did she say what kind?" Trixie asked eagerly.

"Personal, was all. I couldn't get her to say any more. And when I mentioned it to Tom's wife, Celia, she was awfully short with me, so I dropped it." Celia was the upstairs maid and Tom's new bride.

"There's something strange going on," Trixie confided, feeling a rush of curiosity coming back. She told Honey about hearing Regan's parting words to her mother today. "He's certainly worried about something. Tom's probably mixed up in it, and that's why Celia was upset."

Honey nodded. "Maybe Regan's planning to lend them money so they can buy the red trailer they're living in."

"Ugh! I wish they'd buy a house instead and let Di Lynch's father take his old trailer back. Every time I think how close Mart and I came to being kidnaped in that trailer—*br-rr-r!*" Trixie shivered.

"I don't blame you, but Tom and Celia love it," Honey told her. "I've heard Tom say he'd buy it if he could ever raise five thousand dollars to do it. Maybe Regan knows where to get it for him."

"Five thousand! Regan? Where would *he* get that much money? Your dad told mine that when Regan started to work for him a few years ago, he was just out of an orphanage. He couldn't have saved that much."

"I guess not, at that. I heard him tell Miss Trask once that he tried to send money to his sister."

"Anyhow," Trixie knitted her brows, "it wasn't lending money that Regan was so worried about. It was something that might turn out bad and he didn't want us kids to know about it."

"Trixie! Honey!" Mrs. Belden's voice from the foot

of the stairway sounded annoyed. "Dinner is ready and the table isn't even set!"

"Be right down, Moms!" Trixie called out hastily, and as they hurried downstairs, she assured Honey, "We can talk about it later!"

Chapter 3
Suspicions

Outside, the early darkness had settled, but the kitchen of the small farmhouse was warm and cozy as Trixie and Honey came hurrying in from upstairs. Mrs. Belden was taking the roast out of the oven, with Brian's help, and Mart was lounging idly at the end of the sink, watching.

"That's it. You've got it now. Watch out you don't let it slide off the platter," Mart was superintending.

"It's a poor job that can't afford a boss," Trixie confided to Honey loudly, with a nod toward Mart.

Mart snickered. "Come on, small fry. Get moving. It's all we men can do to keep from fainting from starvation. Where's the silverware and stuff? Get crackin', gals!"

Honey giggled and started to pick up the silverware to carry it into the dining-room, but Trixie tossed her head defiantly. "If you're so hungry, why don't you lend Moms a hand, instead of posing around in your new sweater, unconscious?" She flounced into the dining-room with the cups and saucers.

"Me do menial work?" Mart barked after her.

"Seems to me you were the best table-setter at the ranch last Christmas," Honey said mildly, flashing him a smile.

"Hey! So I was!" Mart admitted, sticking out his chest.

"Show Moms how good you were!" Brian laughed, and before Mart could back away, his big brother had deftly brought some hot plates from the warming oven and thrust them into Mart's hands. "Here!"

Mart did an impromptu juggling act trying to keep from dropping the stack of hot plates. "Ow! They're hot!"

Mrs. Belden looked up from decorating the meat platter with tiny sprigs of parsley from her kitchen window garden. "Mart!" she called sternly. "Stop clowning, this minute, and take those plates into the dining-room!"

But Mart was still shifting the plates from one hand to the other, trying to find a cool spot. Brian laughed, and Honey called anxiously, "Don't drop them!"

Mart made a dash for the dining-room but collided with Trixie and lost his grip on the plates. Down they went with a crash.

Mart covered his eyes and turned his head so he wouldn't see the wreckage. "Yipe! There goes my next month's allowance!" he moaned.

Trixie's snicker made him move his hands from his eyes and look around. Nobody seemed worried or shocked. In fact, there were grins on Trixie's and Brian's faces. He stole a quick look at the floor and grunted with surprise.

"Hey, none of them got busted!" he exclaimed.

"Of course not," Trixie's voice was pitying. "Those are Moms's new plastic dishes. They don't break."

"Why didn't somebody tell me that? Here I was getting a nervous breakdown—" Mart was aggrieved.

His mother interrupted. "You'll get worse than that, young man, if you don't pick up those plates, wash and dry them, and get them onto the table by the time Dad comes in and says—"

"When do we eat?" Peter Belden stuck his head in from the dining-room.

The interruption was so well-timed that everyone but Mr. Belden himself broke out laughing, even Mart, who was hurriedly gathering up the plates.

"Did I say something funny?" Mr. Belden asked his wife, perplexed by the reaction.

"Not funny," she laughed. "But you timed it just right. We're ready now, if Brian will carry in the roast. And no more jokes, Brian. Girls, you may bring in the salad and the vegetables."

Bobby was already seated at the table, waiting more or less patiently. He had learned a long time ago to keep out of the kitchen when a meal was being prepared. It was no fun being stepped on or tripped over, and it always seemed to be his fault when it happened, or so Trixie claimed, in spite of his protests.

"I'm starved," he told his parents plaintively. "I got a big empty place and it says *'grr-r-r!'* at me." He patted his fat little stomach soothingly.

"Just a couple of minutes more, lamb," Moms told him. "And we have a big surprise for you. Just watch the door."

Brian marched in and set down the meat platter with a flourish in front of his father.

"Ah!" Mr. Belden beamed down at the roast as he took up his great-grandfather's horn-handled carving set and gave the knife a last whip across the sharpener. "That's what I'd call a fine roast of beef!"

Bobby stared at the meat with a scowl. "If that's the susprise, I like chicken better," he said in an aggrieved voice. "That ol' roast beef doesn't have any drumsticks. An' I *love* drumsticks." He slid down in his chair till only his tip-tilted nose and the scowl showed above the rim of the table.

But a moment later he sat up straight suddenly and

his frown disappeared as he saw Honey coming in from the kitchen carrying a couple of salad dishes. "Hi, Honey!" he sang out joyfully. "I didn' know you were here. You're the susprise!" He looked to his mother eagerly. "C'n Honey sit by me, please?"

"If she wants to," his mother agreed, smiling.

"I'd love it," Honey assured him as she set down the two salad plates and started out for more.

Trixie was coming in with a steaming vegetable dish in each hand. "Ha! Don't forget you'll be stuck to cut up his meat!" she whispered as they dodged around each other without mishap.

"I don't mind. It will be fun," Honey smiled.

"Do it twice a day and three times Saturday and Sunday and you won't think so!" Trixie whispered darkly. Taking care of Bobby was one of her biggest jobs, and she did a lot of grumbling about it, though she didn't really mind it as much as she pretended.

She set down the vegetable dishes where Moms could serve from them, and started back toward the kitchen.

"Trix!" Her father sounded vexed. "What do we eat our food from? The tablecloth? Where are the plates?"

"Coming right up, Dad!" Trixie hurried toward the kitchen door, but the door swung open as Mart came through at the same moment, carrying the plates.

They dodged in first one direction and then the other to avoid another collision. Then Mart, balancing the plates on one hand, firmly shoved her aside. "Step away. We did that routine before, remember?"

Trixie made a face at him and hurried out as Mart set the plates down with a flourish in front of his father. "Here we are," he announced, "washed and dried all spic and span!"

"About time!" Mr. Belden started serving the portions.

It was a lively meal, with a general discussion of the ice carnival plans.

"I wish you B.W.G.'s wouldn't be so stubborn about not accepting financial help. I'm sure the bank would be glad to underwrite part of the expense, for the publicity," Mr. Belden told them.

"Can't, Dad. But they can buy a full-page ad in our souvenir program," Mart said. "We'll be glad to sell any size space desired."

Trixie winked at Honey across the table. Mart was actually volunteering to do one of the hardest jobs connected with the carnival!

"Mart's a wonderful salesman," Trixie assured her father. "The advertising will pay all the expenses. It isn't as if we were raising *money* for something. All we want is donations of books for the library at San Isidro, and people to have a good time, watching our show and trying to win prizes."

"And who donates the prizes?" Mrs. Belden asked.

"Brian will take care of that. I'm sure he won't have any trouble getting the merchants to donate. We'll mention each one in the program."

Brian looked at Mart and Mart looked at Brian. "I just felt a trap snapping shut, didn't you?" Brian asked his brother with a sly wink.

Mart nodded and pretended to look sad. "We're out-maneuvered, son."

"I know what that word means," Trixie grinned.

"You ought to," Mart snapped back at her. "You probably invented it."

"Hey!" Mart interrupted the laughter that his remark had started. "We're due over at the stables. Regan wants to show us how to bandage Thunderer's cut leg so we can change the dressing tomorrow and Sunday."

Usually Jim did the doctoring with Regan, but he wouldn't be back from the field trip until Sunday night.

Mention of Regan's name was all Trixie needed to

get her started puzzling over his visit that afternoon. She simply had to know what it was all about. Maybe Regan would drop some word about it to the boys.

"Why can't Honey and I tag along and watch, too? We ought to know what to do in case one of our horses gets a bad cut sometime out in the woods."

"I suppose we *could* stand their company?" Mart asked Brian gloomily.

"If they don't take too long with the dishes," Brian agreed. "Heaven knows, they have lots to learn."

Honey sighed. "There'll be a sinkful. I guess we can't expect you to wait." She tried to look pathetic.

"Well, see you later, squaws!" Mart started out. "Too bad you're stuck!" He laughed and went out and Brian followed.

"I guess that's that," Trixie sighed as she and Honey gathered up the dishes after Mr. and Mrs. Belden had gone into the living-room to listen to the weather reports.

But a few minutes later, the kitchen door to the hallway opened, and Brian and Mart, bundled up for outdoors, came in.

"Not done yet?" Mart said. "I told you they were slow as molasses!" he told his brother. "Let's go."

But Brian whipped a couple of dish towels off the

rack and handed one to him. "We'll give them a hand."

"Hey! What *is* this? A frame-up?" Mart pretended to be annoyed.

"I think it's darling of you both to help." Honey smiled at them both impartially as she handed them each a plate from the drying rack.

"Okay, we've been outfoxed," Mart groaned, and went to work.

"About the carnival," Brian said over the clatter of silver and dishes. "Are you thinking of a snowman theme or what? We'll have to make up our minds about the theme before we do anything else."

"I've got it!" Trixie splashed a platter into the soapy water so hard in her excitement that suds flew all over. "Mexican! Because it's for the benefit of our Mexican pen pals! And we can wear the Western costumes we got for Tucson! And Jim can sketch some Spanish *señoritas* on the posters for us to color in. . . ."

They talked about it on the way to the Manor House as they plodded along in the starlit night. They each had a flashlight, and they kept pretty well together at first, but Trixie was so anxious to begin talking to Regan that she soon drifted ahead of the others and kept on going when Brian stopped to mend a broken lace on his boot.

She was quite a way ahead of them as she approached the big stables. There was no light in the barn, but the tack-room window showed yellow through the darkness. Regan must be busy there. She headed toward the light.

She heard Regan's big voice as she stepped into the barn. "I know you'll do the best you can, but it's a tricky business and I can't expect miracles. I never thought anything like this could happen."

A man's voice, low-pitched and indistinct, answered. Trixie couldn't make out the words, and the voice didn't sound familiar.

Then Regan spoke again. "Tom and I will get back as early as we can Sunday afternoon and we'll meet at your place. That is, if we have any luck."

Again she heard the murmur of the second man's voice. Regan had referred to Tom, so this wasn't Tom. Who could it be, then? And what kind of "luck" was Regan hoping for?

She decided not to wait for the others. She could hear their voices and laughter outside. She started across the barn toward the partly open tack-room door. The boards in the old floor squeaked loudly, but she was so used to them that she paid no attention.

And as she shoved open the door, the rear half-door

to the stalls was swinging as if someone had just gone out.

"Hi!" she greeted Regan. He was reaching up to turn a knob on the small radio that he kept on the shelf above the harness pegs. He liked to listen to the ball games, in the season, as he worked. He turned up the volume of a musical program before he glanced at her.

"Oh, hello, Trixie. Where are the boys?"

"Coming," she said shortly. "Who was that?" She nodded toward the rear half-door.

"Who was what?" Regan's green eyes looked blank.

"I heard you talking to somebody a minute ago." She was a little surprised. "A man."

"You must have heard me fooling with the radio," Regan said carelessly.

"No," Trixie shook her head. "*You* were talking and I heard this man answering, sort of mumbling. I was just wondering who it was."

"You have a great imagination, young lady," Regan laughed. But his voice sounded sharp a moment later as he added, "Don't let it run away with you. You heard the radio."

Trixie knew that Regan was fibbing deliberately. He just didn't want her to know who was there with him. But why? She felt angry and hurt. Regan had always

41

been so friendly, even when she was dumb about things he tried to show her about riding.

The boys and Honey came in before she could argue any more.

And Regan ignored her pointedly as he led the way to Thunderer's stall and gave the boys a lesson in bandaging. Even Honey noticed how Regan was snubbing Trixie.

"What are you and Regan glaring at each other for?" Honey whispered as Regan demonstrated the way to wrap the injured foreleg.

"Guilty conscience. His, I mean," Trixie whispered back. "Tell you later."

And as they prepared for bed a half hour later, after the chilly walk back from the stables, Trixie explained.

"It isn't at all like Regan," Honey admitted, wrinkling her smooth forehead in perplexity. "Are you *sure* it wasn't the radio, Trixie? You know how you are—"

Trixie glared at her friend. "There you go! I told you I heard *Regan*. I'm certain of it. And the way he acted just now was proof of it. Every time he looked at me he sort of froze up. He thinks I've been spying on him."

"Well—" Honey looked uncomfortable.

Trixie's glare faded. A grin replaced it. "I guess

I can't blame him. I *did* listen, but I didn't intend to."

Honey nodded. "Maybe he's just protecting a friend—the other man you heard. Maybe he's doing something kind for him. Anyhow, it must be all right, or your mother wouldn't have tried to help Regan, would she?"

Trixie sighed. "Of course not! Honey, I'm going to apologize to Regan for being so nosy, and I'm going to forget all about it, no matter what he's up to."

But Honey knew better. Trixie could no more give up trying to solve a mystery—any mystery—than a bulldog could be pried off a bone once he had hold of it!

Chapter 4
The Missing Skate

"T.G.I.S.!" Trixie sat down sleepily at the table and rubbed her eyes.

"M.T.!" Honey agreed, stifling a yawn.

Mr. Belden, who had been up since six doing his weekly home chores, stared at them over the top of his paper. "Translated into English, that means?"

"Thank Goodness It's Saturday!" The two girls laughed, and Honey added, "And I said, 'Me Too!' "

Mr. Belden went back to his paper, shaking his head. But a minute later he put it down quickly as a wail of grief came from the kitchen. "What's the matter with that child? He's done nothing but yell all morning!"

Trixie looked worried. She had overslept again, because she and Honey had talked and giggled half the night. Moms had gotten Bobby up and dressed and down to breakfast without disturbing her and Honey.

"I'll see what I can do," Trixie said hastily.

Her mother and Bobby were looking through the back porch closet for something, among the boots and snowshoes and a stray baseball bat. "Can I help, Moms?" Trixie asked.

"I can't seem to find Bobby's other ice skate. The boys have promised to take him to the lake for another skating lesson this morning as soon as they get back from working out the horses."

"Trixie tooked it! I know she did!" Bobby burst out crying again.

"Look, half-pint!" Trixie held the remaining skate against her shoe. "What good would your skate do me? It's inches too small!"

Bobby looked critically at it and then nodded, dashing away the tears. But they started again at once. "Wah! I'll never find my skate! It's losted!"

Honey came in quickly. "Skate? I think I know where it might be. Last week at the lake, Bobby banged one of his blades against a rock, and Regan took it to the toolhouse to file the nick out of the blade. I imagine the skate is still there, or in the tack room."

"Well, that's a relief!" Mrs. Belden got to her feet. "I imagine Regan's forgotten it, poor fellow."

Trixie felt a tingle along her spine. She had bumped into the mystery again. "Why is he a 'poor fellow,' Moms?" she asked, much too carelessly.

Mrs. Belden looked startled and bit her lip. Then

she gave a little laugh. "I mean he's probably been much too busy taking care of that horse that was cut the other day. He does work hard."

Trixie and Honey looked at each other. Moms wasn't very good at covering up.

She hurried on. "Do you think you could find Bobby's skate at your place, Honey? The boys are still there working with the horses and they can help."

"Of course we'll find it. Come on, Trix and Bobby. And if the skate's all fixed, you and I'll go skating, Bobby, and I'll show you some slick tricks to surprise the boys!"

Bobby was halfway to the door with his lone skate. "Well, come on!"

Trixie hesitated. "I've got a lot to do—" she said, looking almost as pathetic as Bobby had.

Mrs. Belden laughed. "Scoot along. And take your skates. A little bird told me you're going to have to practice hard if you plan to do any fancy stuff at the carnival."

"You can say that again, Moms!" Trixie sighed. "That bird said a beakful, even if he has a blond crew cut and thinks he knows all the answers!"

"He *does,*" Honey laughed, "when it comes to skating, speed skating particularly. Mart's about the nearest to a professional I've ever seen, and Dad's taken me to watch a lot of them."

"Is he that good?" Trixie was really surprised. "Hey, he'll be able to win a prize for the B.W.G.'s. Gleeps, I hope it's something the club can use!"

"Your father thinks his friend Mr. Burnside of the lumber company will donate some flooring from that old salt-box house they're wrecking. It seems to me it would be just right for your clubhouse," Moms said.

"That's it! We'll ask Mr. Maypenny how to lay it. And we won't have everything getting dusty the way it does." Trixie was planning. "Y'know, that salt-box house was famous. Maybe we could charge admission to show the floor. . . ."

"Dad hasn't even spoken to Mr. Burnside yet," her mother reminded her. "Remember that old saying about not counting your chickens before they're hatched!"

"My skate!" Bobby interrupted, tugging at Honey's hand. "Bundle me up an' let's go."

"A good idea. Scoot, all of you!" Mrs. Belden shook her apron at them, smiling. And they scooted to dress in their heavy sweaters and scarves.

"You're spoiling those youngsters." Mr. Belden was in the doorway, newspaper in hand. "They should do their chores first. They're old enough to feel responsible."

"I know." Mrs. Belden smiled saucily at her husband. "I'm terrible. I make rules and then break them." She walked over to the hall door and watched a moment as Trixie and Honey and Bobby shrugged into their outdoor clothing and left hastily, laughing and talking.

Mrs. Belden turned and saw her husband's affectionate smile. "But I'm not sorry. They're so young and so—helpless." She hesitated a little over the last word.

Peter Belden snorted and rattled his paper. "Trixie and Honey helpless? After the situations they've managed to get into and out of again without getting hurt?"

"I guess I wasn't thinking of them, so much. They're lucky—about a lot of things. But there are others who may not mean any more harm at the start than our girls do, but who've had a different kind of luck."

Mr. Belden looked serious. "I know. Poor Regan. I wish we could do more to help him, but the safest thing is to stay out of it and hope it works out."

The wind was blowing hard as Trixie and Honey ventured out into Glen Road, each holding one of Bobby's hands. Big racing clouds were moving down from the Catskills. Soft and fluffy like great gobs of swirling whipped cream, they seemed to be trying to escape the masses of dark gray that pursued and swallowed them one by one.

"Looks like another big one," Honey shouted against the roar of the wind.

"Marvelous! Hope the snow sticks around till we've staged our carnival!" Trixie yelled back. "It would be gloopy if the lake defrosted too soon!"

Now they were past the woods that divided Crabapple Farm from the Wheeler estate. The neat little cottage at the foot of the long sloping driveway had once been the gatehouse of the Manor House. The B.W.G.'s had taken it over as their clubhouse.

Trixie and Honey had found it last summer, veiled and almost hidden by rank-growing wild honeysuckle and wisteria vines. Now, thanks to a great deal of effort on the part of all the Bob-Whites, it stood neat and strong in its grove with blue spruce and dogwood trees all around.

There had been mystery around the cottage at first, about a stolen diamond imbedded in the dirt floor, and vicious thieves who wanted it. But Trixie and Honey had outmaneuvered them and turned them over to the law.

Later, in a November hurricane, a tree had smashed the roof in. But with hard work, they had restored it, weathertight. Now all their summer and winter sports equipment, from water skis to toboggans, was stored safely in it.

They stopped to admire their clubhouse, ignoring Bobby's impatient tugging.

"It was worth the struggle," Trixie said solemnly.

"And lots of fun," Honey added.

"It was a good thing Mr. Maypenny showed the boys how to put on the new roof," Trixie giggled, "though he did do most of the heavy work himself, so he'd be sure it would be done right."

"Our brothers didn't mind that a bit!" Honey laughed. "Remember how you and I thought the old dear was a big, bad poacher, robbing Dad's game preserve—"

Trixie nodded. "I sure do."

"Well, he's a wonderful gamekeeper, and Brian calls him a typical Hudson River Valley settler and salt of the earth."

"I'm c-cold and I want my skate!" Bobby pulled at her sleeve. "Why do we stand here talking?"

"That's a fair question, Bobby," Honey admitted. "Let's race Trixie up to the stables, hey? Come on!"

She took Bobby's hand and they started running up the long driveway, but Trixie didn't accept the challenge. Let 'em run. She had some thinking to do, about Regan and his mysterious problem. Moms had almost come out with it. Some kind of trouble. Maybe he had had an accident, hit-and-run or something. But Regan would never run. He would stay and face it, whatever had happened. Maybe it was Tom who was in a jam. Maybe his wife Celia would let something drop about it. Maybe she would mention that stranger who was in the tack room last night with Regan.

She caught herself suddenly. She had told Honey she wasn't going to think about it any more, and here she was all tangled up in it in her mind.

"I'm going to forget it!" she said fiercely, out loud, and then started up the driveway, running to overtake Honey and Bobby, and put this silly mystery out of her mind.

Honey and Bobby, flushed and breathless, were waiting outside the barn. "Let's do it again!" Bobby called out.

"Not me! You won fair and square!" Trixie laughed and winked at Honey.

"The boys—don't seem to be—around," Honey panted. "Guess they're still riding."

"We can look around the tack room for Angel Face's skate, and ask them when they come if they've seen it any place."

So they went into the tack room and looked high and low. "Not here," Trixie decided, lifting aside a paper file box to look behind it.

As she picked up the file box, the unfastened end of it dropped open. A pile of bills and papers slid out onto the shelf and some fluttered to the floor.

"Gleeps! Now I've done it!" Trixie moaned. "Look, Honey! Regan will skin me alive. I've spilled all his bills and stuff, and I don't know how he had them filed."

Honey came over swiftly. "Let's pick them up and put them in the file, and when we see him tomorrow, we can explain that it was an accident."

They retrieved most of the papers, but one sheet had drifted under the workbench. Trixie had to crawl after it.

"I hope he won't be too angry." She wriggled out backward clutching the missing sheet. "Here, slip this in—" She broke off abruptly and stared at the writing on it.

"Now what?" Honey asked, seeing her expression.

"A page from a letter—" Trixie still stared at the paper. She read, aloud, " '—but Judge Armen is willing to let you try. Your sister felt it was probably the last hope left to straighten—' Oh! I'm sorry!" Trixie's face was scarlet as she thrust the paper at Honey. "Here, put it away!"

Honey slipped it into the file and replaced the file on the shelf. "You didn't mean to snoop, Trix."

"I really am sorry," Trixie confessed unhappily.

"You couldn't help glancing at it," Honey insisted. "It was perfectly natural. Anyhow, you only read a few words. You didn't find out anything you shouldn't."

Trixie sighed. "But I did, Hon. It practically said that Regan's in some kind of trouble with the law."

There were voices outside at that moment, and the sound of horses' hoofs on the barn floor. The boys had returned.

Bobby ran out to meet them. "We can't find my skate," the girls heard him complain loudly. "Have you got it?"

"Honey," Trixie still felt terribly guilty, "we don't have to tell them about Regan being in trouble, do we?"

Honey looked grave and shook her head. "We would just be gossiping if we did. I still say you didn't find out anything, really. So there's nothing we *could* tell."

But Trixie wasn't so sure. And now she had a new worry. Maybe Regan hadn't told Miss Trask the truth when she sent him to Moms for advice. Maybe he wasn't as honest as he had always seemed. She knew that he hadn't told her the truth about having someone in the tack room with him last night.

She decided not to say any more to Honey or anyone. She would just keep an eye on Regan when he came back, and if she got any evidence that he was up to something, she would tell Moms and Dad right away. "But I still hope I'm all wrong," she told herself.

Chapter 5
Bobby's See-Crud

"You don't wanna find my skate," Bobby sniffed indignantly. "You're not lookin'!" He pulled at his sister's sleeve.

"Oh, Bobby, stop pestering! We're helping the boys so we can all go skating together. We'll be finished in a few minutes, and then we'll look for your skate!" Trixie was currycombing Strawberry while Honey attended to sleek Starlight in the next stall. Mart and Brian were measuring out the horses' next meal and cleaning the leather.

"We have several of the antique sale posters laid away in the clubhouse," Brian called out to Trixie as he went past. "Why can't we use the reverse side of them for our carnival announcements?"

"Swell idea," Trixie agreed at once.

Mart glanced over the top of the next stall at Honey, working hard grooming Starlight. "When's Jim due home? Did he have any idea?"

"Late tomorrow, he said," Honey answered cheerfully. "Won't he be thrilled when he hears all the plans we've made?"

"Yeah, especially when he finds out he's booked to draw posters, help build the booths, run off the programs on the school printing press—if he can get permission, of course—and—" Mart was ticking off the items on his fingers.

"—and see that certain parties don't hand him *all* the jobs and just go around talking big about how hard they are working!" Trixie finished the sentence saucily.

"Where did Bobby go?" Brian asked suddenly, as he was getting ready to take care of Thunderer's cut leg. "Hey, Bobby! Where are you?" he called. Then he put aside the bandages to stride outside and look around.

Trixie groaned. Instead of helping with the horses, a job she really liked, she should have been keeping an eye on Bobby. She hurried outside to Brian.

He was looking up and down the driveway for Bobby. "Here." She tossed Strawberry's currycomb to him. "I'll try the house. He may have decided to mooch some cookies at the kitchen."

Trixie hurried up toward the Manor House, calling impatiently first in one direction and then the other, "Bobby! Where are you?"

She was about halfway to the Manor House when she saw the little boy come around the corner from the rear, with Miss Trask on one side and Celia on the other.

He was carrying a skate in one hand while he munched on a fistful of cookies from his other hand.

He waved gaily. "Hi, Trixie! We founded my skate!" he called, and came running.

The gray-haired house supervisor and Celia halted to watch him greet Trixie, and then they turned and went back to the house with a farewell wave.

"Tom fixed it, Celia says. It was in the kitchen. Now can we go skating?" Bobby ran the words all together.

"I guess so, if it doesn't snow too hard," Trixie told him, holding firmly to his wrist as they went back to the barn. "Let's see what Brian says."

The work was finished, and they quickly decided that half an hour on the ice would do them all a lot of good. They set out, stopping only a few minutes at the clubhouse to get their skates.

It was quite a distance into the woods before they would come to the lake. They went single file through the evergreen forest to the sloping hillside that sheltered one end of the lake from the heavier wind. There was a good spot among the rocks where they always built a campfire, and the boys went to work at once to get one started.

The ice was smooth and clean. Honey put her skates on at once and checked to see that there were no broken twigs imbedded in the ice in the little cove where she planned to take Bobby for his skating lesson.

Trixie and Mart paced off a length of shoreline along which Mart intended to work up his speed. They marked it with a strip of red cloth at each end, and Mart went to work practicing, while Brian held the watch on him.

Trixie was feeding the campfire with some wood she had gathered, when Honey started to the cove with Bobby by the hand.

"You can come 'n' watch, Trixie," Bobby called to his sister as he skated more or less steadily at Honey's side.

"All right. You practice a while, and I'll be with you soon," she called, waving them on.

She was still feeding the fire carefully a few minutes later, when she heard the sound of a car's motor. It was coming from the private road over on the other side of the hill.

It was a steep, narrow road and very bumpy. It wasn't meant for anything but a four-wheel-drive car, and from the sound of this car, the driver was having a time getting uphill with this one. The road led only to the game preserve and Mr. Maypenny's cabin in the center of it.

She knew that Mr. Maypenny didn't have a car. In fact, he positively loathed the "critters." When he didn't walk on his rounds of the traps and snares for the pesty little jack rabbits, he rode Brownie, his old mare.

Now the chugging and puffing sounded as if it were just on the other side of the hill. Trixie couldn't resist climbing up to the top of the hill among the tall spruces and trying to see who was driving that car. If it turned out to be Mr. Maypenny himself, she would have fun teasing him about driving, after all the things he had said about cars.

She started to climb, but she was in too much of a hurry. She carelessly stepped on a loose rock on the side of the hill and stumbled, landing on one knee. It was a hard fall and it hurt; by the time she had scrambled to her feet and limped the rest of the way up to the top of the hill, the car had passed. The only glimpse she had of it was of the rear end turning a corner in the road and going out of sight.

She rubbed her painfully skinned knee and went down the hill again, very much annoyed with herself.

The storm had really begun now, and the wind was sending heavy gusts of snow across the surface of the ice.

Brian and Mart were waiting beside the fire. "Let's

call it a day," Brian said, glancing at the lead-colored sky.

Honey was coming across the ice, with Bobby at her side, and the wind was blowing them unmercifully.

"I only falled down once," Bobby boasted as they came up to the fire.

"Good for you, young feller!" Mart laughed. "Now how about heading for home?"

"But I'm c-cold," Bobby complained, and huddled shivering at the fire.

"Let him get warmed through first, and then we'll come along after you," Honey told the boys.

"I'll wait with you," Trixie said hastily. She was glad to linger so the boys wouldn't have a chance to notice that she was limping. She knew that Mart would tease her about it.

"Okay, but don't wait too long," Brian glanced skyward again. "This one looks like a meanie."

"And stomp out the fire, squaws," Mart added. "With this wind, one live spark could make a lot of animals homeless—and lifeless!"

"To say nothing of Mr. Maypenny," Brian said grimly. "So don't forget."

Trixie's knee was hurting and it made her cross. "Go on ahead. I guess we're as good woodsmen as you two. We know what we're doing." She was trying to stand very straight but if they didn't hurry and start off, she just knew she was going to collapse.

"Hey!" Mart pointed to her knee. "What's with the torn dungarees? Did you 'falled down,' too?"

"Go on, and stop asking silly questions!" Trixie gripped the slim trunk of a sapling beside her and held on. "You didn't see the ice cracked anywhere, did you?"

Brian laughed and drew Mart away with him. "See you later at the clubhouse, ladies."

As soon as they were out of sight, Trixie groaned and sat down on a flat rock, gingerly feeling the injured knee.

"Why, you did fall, didn't you?" Honey hurried to her. "Let me see."

Trixie had tucked her dungarees into the top of her boots, so they had to pull off the boot before they could roll up the pants leg and look at the scraped spot. Trixie fingered it gently, with a moan or two, and then decided that nothing was broken after all. "Just a scrape," she told Honey.

"We'll get the first-aid kit at the clubhouse and bandage you pretty," Honey told her, "with some of that red, white, and blue adhesive tape."

"I want some heap-o'-tape, too. See?" Bobby held out a finger with a tiny scratch on it. "I hurt awful."

Trixie grinned at him as she rolled down her pants leg. "We'll put some on the other hand, too, so you'll balance!"

Bobby's eyes shone. "I love you, Trixie!" He flung his arms around Trixie's neck, and they hugged each other.

"But you must promise not to tell Mart or Brian that I skinned my knee," Trixie warned him. "That's our secret."

"I love see-cruds," Bobby nodded happily. "I know a see-crud."

"What is it, doll?" Trixie kept her arm around him and winked at Honey, who was smiling at them both. "A big, big secret?"

"Uh-huh," Bobby nodded and looked serious. "It's Miss Trask's see-crud, an' Celia's, an' it's about Regan an' Tom, an'—"

Trixie put her free hand over his mouth to stop him. "Then you mustn't tell it to me if it belongs to them."

Bobby pulled her hand away so he could speak, and backed off. "It's somethin' Regan's bringing home from the city!" he shouted at Trixie. "It's a big sperimen! What's a sperimen, Honey?"

"A sperimen?" Honey looked bewildered. "I never heard of a sperimen."

"Neither did I," Trixie laughed. "There's no such thing, Bobby."

Bobby's face was red and his eyes blazed. "Is so!" he shouted at his sister. "Miss Trask says it's a danger-ish sperimen, so there! Maybe it's a—a snake!" He was not happy with the idea and shivered as he stood staring at them.

Honey laughed. "I never heard of a snake by that name. And anyhow, both Tom and Regan hate snakes, so there's no chance your sperimen is a snake."

The two girls exchanged glances over Bobby's head, and then Trixie touched her knee and said, "Ouch! That scrape hurts. I think we'd better be getting back to the clubhouse. How about putting out the fire, if every-body's warm enough now?" She looked meaningly at Bobby.

"Let me!" Bobby started kicking the damp snow onto the fire and tramping it into the earth to put out any last embers. It was one task he loved, and he did it very efficiently.

The girls waited and watched to see that he didn't overlook any half-burned sticks.

"What do you suppose he meant by *sperimen*, Trix?" Honey whispered.

"Sperimen. Sperimen." Trixie whispered the word

to herself. "Hey, do you suppose she said *experiment?*"

Honey laughed. "That's probably just what she did say. But goodness knows what she meant! And anyhow, I guess it's none of our business."

"I guess not." Trixie sighed. "But this trip of Regan's is getting 'curiouser and curiouser' as Alice in Wonderland said. What kind of an experiment would he bring home?"

But it was foolish to stand there in the darkening woods while the wind whipped snow in their faces. So they hurried off after Bobby, and Trixie found her injured knee getting better as she thought less and less of how much it hurt.

In fact, the three of them reached the clubhouse a lot sooner than they had expected to, and they were happy to find the cheerful little stove sending out warmth that felt pretty good after the hike.

Mart and Brian had found the old posters, discovered that they would do nicely for the new project, and had laid them out on the conference table, with pots of paint and clean brushes, so nothing would delay Jim from going to work on them when he got back from his field trip.

Brian looked up from the table. "Hey, I hear a car."

"Maybe Dad and Mother changed their minds and

came back," Honey guessed happily and ran to open the door.

The snow was falling rather heavily now, and the car that had turned into the sloping driveway was having trouble starting up the steep grade.

Trixie looked over Honey's shoulder, and Bobby peered past them. "It's your mom's old car," Trixie said. "Isn't that the one Regan and Tom took into town?"

Honey nodded, disappointed, and started to close the door. "They're back a lot sooner than they expected."

"Where's the sperimen?" Bobby shrilled at the car.

The windows were rolled up and Tom, the driver, didn't hear. He kept his attention on the now slippery road and went on up the driveway.

But before the door closed out the sound of the car laboring up the hilly drive, Trixie recognized the choking and sputtering of the motor.

There was no doubt about it. This car of Honey's mother's was the same car that she had heard an hour ago climbing the rough, narrow road beyond the lake hill.

Chapter 6
The New Pupil

Of course, Trixie admitted to herself, it was possible that she was just imagining that the car she had heard out by the lake was the same one that had just coughed and sputtered its way past the clubhouse with Tom at the wheel.

She decided that she wouldn't say anything about it to the boys. She would feel pretty silly if she had and then Regan denied that he had been out near the lake today. He had been annoyed enough last night when she had tried to find out who had been talking to him in the tack room. She still had to tell him about having spilled the contents of his letter file. If he suspected that she had read part of his letter—wow! He might get angry enough with her to tell the Wheelers that she had been prying into his private affairs.

Brian had drawn a rough map of the lake, and he and Mart had their heads together over it, trying to decide just where the booths should be for the carnival and where to stage the ice show.

"Keep everything in the lee of the hill where the wind won't hit," Mart advised.

"And be sure to have one booth for hot chocolate and coffee—" Honey reminded them.

"An' ice cream." Bobby clapped his hands. "An' tell Regan to bring the sperimen."

"The what?" Mart looked to the girls for an explanation.

"He means experiment," Honey laughed. "Bobby thinks Regan's brought home some kind of an experiment, and he is hoping it isn't a snake!"

"Not this time of year, Bobby," Brian explained to his small brother gravely. "The snakes all go into their little nests under the big rocks and they go to sleep till the ground warms up again. They don't like ice and snow."

"Oh!" Bobby seemed relieved. He knew that anything Brian said was true. He couldn't always depend on Mart or Trixie. They liked to tease him. "I'm glad."

"You see? Honey told you!" Trixie laughed. "Nobody ever heard of a sperimen snake."

"Oh." Bobby smiled at Honey. "I thought it was *you* said so, Trixie."

"Ha!" Mart chuckled. "Talk about casting aspersions on a certain person's veracity!"

Trixie gave him a withering glance and hooked her arm in Honey's. "I hope that dictionary you swallowed gives you indigestion, smarty pants. Come on, Honey, let's leave the uncouth savages!" And she added, with a Western twang, "Come along, gal, and help Moms rustle up some grub for the hands!"

"Ki-yi-yippy-ay-yay!" Mart gave a cowboy yodel as the girls snatched up their jackets and scarves and hurried toward the door. "Hey, where you going so fast? Are you leaving Little Tornado on our hands?"

Trixie sighed. "I wouldn't think of it. Come on, Bobby." And in spite of his wriggles and protests, she and Honey had him zipped into his overcoat in a few seconds and were on their way home along Glen Road.

After the first few unwilling yards, he began running ahead, cheerfully kicking up the fallen snow and trying to catch the new flakes in his mouth as he ran.

Trixie and Honey followed at a more dignified pace, arm in arm, enjoying the gentle touch of the snowflakes on their pink cheeks and pinker noses.

"I could hardly wait to tell you," Trixie confided, "but I'm almost sure that Regan went up to see Mr. Maypenny today before he came home. Maybe Mr. Maypenny knows about the experiment, whatever it is."

Honey was surprised. "What makes you think Regan went to see him?" she asked, and her hazel eyes got wider and wider as Trixie told about hearing the car.

"What on earth could the experiment be about?" Honey frowned.

Trixie shrugged. "Well, whatever it was, it didn't take Regan and Tom very long to take care of it in town. I hope it's all fixed up now."

And a few minutes later, as she and Honey and Bobby all tramped into the kitchen, it seemed that it *had* been "fixed up." Mrs. Belden was talking to Miss Trask on the phone.

"I'm so glad to hear it," she was saying. "It appeared to me that that was the best thing for Regan to do, and I'm glad he decided to try it. It's too bad we can't do more, but we have to think of how the others might—" She broke off abruptly as Trixie came in with Honey. Then she went on, lightly, "But I must stop gabbing. My starving infants have just arrived and I'm afraid they'll have to be fed." After a few more laughing remarks, she hung up the receiver.

The others? Trixie thought. *Wonder if that means us?* But she knew better than to ask her mother.

"Has Miss Trask heard from Dad and Mother?" Honey asked her hostess eagerly.

"As a matter of fact, that's why she called, dear. They won't be home for ten days or so, and if you wish, you may stay right here with us till Jim gets back from his field trip," Mrs. Belden smiled, "or longer."

So it was arranged, and both Trixie and Honey were delighted. They had so much to talk about, anyhow, that they would have been on the phone for hours every day if Honey hadn't been under the same roof.

By Monday morning, after much conferring in the clubhouse, the Bob-Whites had set the date for their ice carnival. Honey, who was a whiz at sewing, had already sketched a few of the Spanish costumes they would wear; and Trixie had chewed the ends off two perfectly good pencils trying to figure how they could raise cash to buy the materials for the costumes.

She was moaning about it as she and Honey and Di Lynch waited in the chilly wind that morning for the school bus.

Di, the other member of the B.W.G.'s, had been helping a lot. It was her Uncle Monty's dude ranch at which they had spent the Christmas holidays in Tucson. Di owned several Mexican shawls and high tortoise-shell combs and some red-heeled dancing slippers that Uncle Monty had sent to his sister, Di's mother, when she had given a New Year's Ball. Di had good news for the girls.

"Mother says we can use all of that stuff. And lots

more Indian and Mexican pottery and serapes that Uncle Monty sent for decorations. We'll have all the booths draped with them," Diana planned. "And I've written Uncle Monty to send us a whole lot of cactus candy to sell in one of the booths."

"Cactus candy? Ugh! I should think people would choke on all those awful spines!" Trixie shuddered.

"They peel the cactus before they make the candy out of it." Di laughed. "Not a choke in a carload!"

Mart and Brian had caught the early bus because they expected to do a bit of preliminary advertising among their classmates about the carnival.

"I hope we picked a good date for our show," Trixie said. "It would be horrible if it snowed hard and all our customers stayed home. I'd die if we had to write to Dolores and Lupe and tell them we had had a flop."

"What we need is a good old-fashioned almanac." Honey laughed. "Mr. Lytell has one in his store that he swears by. He reads every word in it, and he insists that it never misses telling exactly what kind of weather to expect every day of the year."

"I saw one of those in Mr. Maypenny's kitchen, the day he gave us that stew for lunch when we barged in on him," Trixie said, her blue eyes sparkling suddenly with an idea. "Hey! Why don't we ride out there after school

73

and ask him to show us what the weather's going to be like on the twenty-seventh? If it's supposed to be sleet-and-snowy, we can change the date before the posters are dated!"

"Why go all that way?" Honey's own eyes twinkled. She knew Trixie. "We can stop by Mr. Lytell's store and ask to look at his almanac."

"I'd rather ask Mr. Maypenny," Trixie said promptly. "Mr. Lytell's always so grouchy. Besides, we have to ride Susie and Starlight this afternoon anyhow."

Honey grinned at her friend. "And besides, you think you might get Mr. Maypenny to tell you what kind of experiment Regan's doing. You still think it was Mother's car you heard by the lake!" She spoke low so Di wouldn't hear. Di was greeting another schoolmate a few feet away.

Trixie had the grace to blush. "Well," she pouted, "I guess I do, really. And it would be fun to know."

The bus came just then, so nothing was settled. They climbed aboard the bus and the three girls went on back to the rear seats that they usually took.

But the bus driver didn't close the door at once. He seemed to be waiting for someone. Trixie noticed it. She craned her neck to look through the windshield.

"We must have a new rider," she told Di and Honey.

A moment later, a boy who looked about Mart's age came up the step. He had a thin, dark face, and was wearing a peaked black cap with a patent-leather band, and a broad-shouldered black leather jacket with the collar turned up. His black eyes peered out from under the shiny visor of the cap and swept the length of the bus, almost as if he expected to see some danger there. His face was grim and unsmiling.

Trixie kicked Honey in the ankle, and out of the side of her mouth she whispered, "Wonder where he left his motorcycle."

The boy's eyes fixed on Trixie almost as if he had heard what she was saying. They were cold eyes and not in the least friendly.

Trixie swallowed hard, and her face got red. She knew the stranger couldn't have heard her, but there was no doubt that he had read her expression and resented it.

She gasped, a moment later, as a second person came up the bus steps close behind the boy, and dropped two fares into the driver's box.

It was Mr. Maypenny, dressed in "store clothes." He didn't look at all comfortable in them. The shirt collar seemed to be choking him, and he had evidently put on some weight since he had last worn the suit, because the coat was open and it was easy to see that it couldn't possibly be buttoned.

Mr. Maypenny glanced toward the rear of the bus, and both Trixie and Honey smiled and waved to him. But he merely nodded briefly and looked back toward the boy with him. "Sit down." He pointed to a seat up close to the driver, and when the boy had silently obeyed, Mr. Maypenny sat down beside him and faced forward as the bus started toward Sleepyside.

"For goodness' sake, where did he find that?" Trixie whispered. She could still feel the sting of the look the strange boy had given her.

Honey, her eyes still on them, looked puzzled. "Maybe it's somebody who's going to help him with the work. I heard Dad say a couple of times that Mr. Maypenny needed a helper, especially in the winter, when the feeding stations have to be filled so often for the deer. It's too much work for one man alone."

"He doesn't look like an outdoor character to me," Trixie sniffed. "That black leather jacket! Ugh! I expected to see some crazy club name on the back of it when he sat down!"

"That's strange." Honey looked startled. "I did, too!" Then she giggled. "I guess we've seen too many movies!"

Trixie nodded and grinned. Then she frowned. "You know, I get the funniest feeling about him. I feel as if I had seen him before somewhere. And still, I know I haven't."

She was still puzzling about it when the bus arrived at Sleepyside High and everyone got out. Mr. Maypenny and the boy headed directly toward the principal's office, without stopping to speak to the girls.

"It looks as if Mr. Maypenny's friend is going to enroll in our school," Di said, as the three strolled toward their home room. "He's sort of good-looking, isn't he?"

Trixie sniffed. "Thr-r-rilling, I'm sure!"

Di looked hurt, but Honey laughed and patted her arm. "Don't mind Trixie. She's just teasing you. She thinks he's stunning."

Trixie flashed her friend a reproachful look and stalked away with her nose high. She *didn't* like the strange boy, no matter what Honey or Di thought about him. And she wished that she could think of whom it was that he reminded her!

Chapter 7
The Rebel

By lunch time there was scarcely a cloud left in the sky. The storm had swept south, leaving only a few inches of soft new snow in the valley, but the air from the north was cold and crisp. It made the girls step along briskly on their way to the cafeteria.

"Feels good," Trixie said happily. "No signs of a thaw. I hope it keeps up this way."

They had filled their lunch trays at the cafeteria counter and taken them to the usual table in one corner of the lunchroom, when they saw Mart come in with the new pupil.

"Look at what's coming with Mart!" Trixie whispered. "Our friend!"

Di Lynch and Brian had sat down a few moments earlier and had started to eat. "Why the whispering, Miss Sherlock Holmes?" Brian asked. Then he caught the direction of their eyes, and he stared also.

Most of the other pupils either stared openly or took furtive glances at the newcomer. Mart saw it and his face reddened, but he continued to lead the new boy toward the table where his friends were sitting.

Now that Trixie could get a full look at the newcomer, she was less impressed by him than before. He was wearing the black leather jacket and had his cap tucked under his arm, but the thing that made her gasp was the style of shoes he was wearing. She hadn't noticed them at the bus. They were cowboy boots.

She craned her neck to be sure she was seeing right. There was no mistake. They were pointed-toe boots with a high heel, and they were black and highly polished.

Mart and the dark boy were at the table now. "Hi, family and such! This is Dan Mangan. Dan, here are some of the characters you'll have to put up with in Sleepyside High."

Brian was cordial. He rose and shook hands solemnly with Dan Mangan, and the solemn-faced Dan managed a smile and a brief "Hi," in return.

But in spite of Honey's quick smile and Di's admiring look, Dan only nodded stiffly to the girls. "As if it hurt him to be polite," Trixie whispered as Mart and Dan went to the counter to get trays and serve themselves.

"He's just bashful," Di guessed and fluffed her soft black curls around her neck.

"Huh!" Trixie noticed the curl-fluffing with a critical eye. "You can call it that, but it looks more like just plain old rude, to me."

"Trixie Belden, you're not being fair," Honey told her quietly. "You don't know a thing about the poor fellow, and you're deciding not to like him."

"Oh, it's just that black leather jacket, I guess," Trixie answered truthfully. "And those cowboy boots. Why would anybody wear cowboy boots?"

"Maybe it's a club outfit, like our red jackets," Honey guessed. "When he walked away just now, the sun hit the back of his jacket through that window. And I'm almost sure I saw where something had been painted over, right in the middle of the back."

"Really? What did it say?" Trixie was interested now.

"I couldn't tell. But I bet it was the name of some club he belongs to," Honey told them.

Di's eyes were wide. "I saw a movie about a street gang that wore black leather jackets. They were awful. Always fighting. Do you think he's like that?" She was ready to be alarmed as she stared at Dan and Mart coming across the cafeteria with their trays loaded.

Trixie saw Di's expression and was suddenly ashamed of herself. She told Di hastily, "He's probably a very nice guy. And either Mr. Maypenny has hired him to help on the preserve, like Honey suggested, or else he's Mr. Maypenny's grandson."

"Grandson, I bet!" Honey guessed enthusiastically. "He's probably been living in the city all his life. That's why he's so thin, maybe. And Mr. Maypenny's hoping to fatten him up with country air and some of his wonderful cooking."

"Got it all figured out, haven't you?" Brian laughed. "Now how about eating lunch before the assembly bell rings?" But even he stopped eating and looked surprised as Mart came on alone after introducing Dan Mangan to three ninth graders at the next table. Dan was setting down his tray there and seating himself.

Mart met their inquiring looks a little sheepishly as he emptied his tray and sat down with them. "Dan's getting acquainted with the guys in our home room," he explained. "It's better."

Di pouted and glanced at the empty chair next to her own. "Who needs him?" she asked. "Would have crowded us anyhow!"

But Trixie, holding back an impish grin, kicked Honey's ankle under the table and winked knowingly. Di was miffed, and Trixie knew it. That came of being so pretty that everybody swooned over you. When they didn't, it was a blow.

It was getting crowded in the lunchroom, and everyone was talking louder and louder. Over at the next table, Dan had an audience of three who were hanging on his every word. "Sure," he said carelessly, toying with his food and waving his fork to emphasize his words, "I helped start our club. Nobody tells us what to do around our neighborhood. We take care of that!" There was a pause and then he went on. "Switch blades? Not us! The cops get tough when they find 'em on you. We don't need stuff like that." He struck a fist into the palm of his other hand forcefully. "Pow!"

His audience had forgotten to eat. All three pairs of eyes were fixed on Dan.

Trixie turned to her brother. "How did you get stuck to take him around?" she asked with a nod in Dan's direction.

"Aw, he's okay. Just feeling his way. He'll calm down," Mart laughed. "Mr. Maypenny asked Miss Taylor if I could introduce him around."

"Hmph!" Trixie snorted. "He seems to be doing pretty well by himself." She eyed Dan speculatively. "Did she say he was related to Mr. Maypenny?"

"Yeah," Mart said, suddenly aware that the other two girls were listening. "I'll tell you the whole terrible story, gals. Well, it seems that Dan was kidnaped by gypsies when he was a baby, and now he's the real king of the gypsies, but there's another band of gypsies who are out to s-s-slit his gullet—" He was whispering, and he made a funny gurgling noise and ran his finger suggestively across his throat as he spoke.

Di gave a horrified exclamation, and Honey's hazel eyes looked like saucers, but Trixie knew her brother better than they did.

"So he's hiding out in Sleepyside," she chimed in with a twinkle in her china-blue eyes, "till he can rally an army and march against his enemies. And in the meantime, he's working for Mr. Maypenny to raise the money to pay for his army!"

Mart put up his hands in token of surrender. "You win!" he laughed. "I surrender!"

And while both Honey and Di Lynch still looked a little bewildered, the bell rang to warn them all that it was time to get back to their classes.

After school, Trixie and Honey went to the Wheeler stable to get their horses.

"I hate to see Regan," Trixie sighed as they sighted the broad-shouldered, red-haired groom at work near the stalls. "I've got to tell him about spilling his letter file, and I know he'll snap my head off."

But to her amazement, Regan was friendly, and

he even laughed when she reluctantly admitted her accident.

"It was pretty well mixed up, as it was," he said good-naturedly. "Forget it."

He helped them saddle up, and while he did, he asked Honey, "Did you know that Maypenny finally hired somebody to help him take care of the game preserve?"

"We saw a boy with him, a dark boy named Dan Mangan," Honey told him. "He seems very nice, but he doesn't look very strong."

Regan hesitated. Then he laughed, "He's probably one of those stringy ones that are a lot stronger than they look."

Trixie couldn't keep out of it. "He was telling some of the boys at school about belonging to a tough gang in the city. I bet he was just putting it on."

Regan's face flushed, and he hesitated even longer this time before he answered. "Well, Trixie, a lot of people talk big because they think other people will like them better. Maybe Danny Mangan's like that."

Honey nodded quickly. "I know how it is, Trix. I used to be scared of the water, till a girl at the boarding school where I used to go laughed at me and told everyone I was afraid. So the next day at the pool I jumped right in, though I was sure I'd drown. And the first thing I knew, I was swimming."

"And now you're the prize swimmer of the Bob-Whites," Trixie added admiringly.

Regan nodded sagely. "That's how it goes. This boy Danny, now, he's taking a job he doesn't know anything about, and going into a school where he doesn't know a living soul. He's got to put up a good front, hasn't he?"

"That's right," Trixie agreed. And Honey nodded.

"Well?" Regan grinned.

"But he *is* Mr. Maypenny's grandson, isn't he?" Trixie flung the question at him suddenly as she settled into her saddle.

Regan frowned. "Where did you get that?"

"Why, I don't know—we were just kind of guessing," Trixie said hurriedly. "There's no reason why he should be, except—I guess we were just hoping he was, because Mr. Maypenny doesn't seem to have anybody."

Regan laughed, and the sharpness was gone out of his voice again as he told her, "If you ask me, he's pretty satisfied without relations. Most of the time all you get from relations is grief." He went on back into the stables, whistling.

"I still think—" Trixie wrinkled her forehead.

"Come on, stop thinking! If Dan Mangan *were* Mr. Maypenny's grandson, there'd be no reason why Regan wouldn't say so. So he isn't. And anyhow, what difference does it make to us? Or to Susie and Starlight, who are chewing their bits like mad!"

They cantered off down the driveway and along Glen Road to the pathway up into the woods.

"I guess whatever was worrying Regan is all right now," Trixie said after they had slowed down for the climb up the narrow trail to the game preserve.

"You sound almost sorry!" her best friend said with a giggle.

"I'm not, really," Trixie said soberly. "I'm glad. Only—if it *was* something so important that he had to ask Miss Trask and Moms what to do about it, how could it all be cleared up in a teeny-weeny little trip to the city? And I still wonder what it meant in the letter about a judge—"

"Oh, dear, I thought you were going to forget about that letter!"

Trixie sighed and flushed. "I'm trying to. Honest!"

Honey reined in suddenly. "Look up ahead!" she said quietly.

Startled, Trixie reined in Susie and shielded her eyes from the slanting beam of sunlight coming down past the snow-laden trees. "Dan Mangan. And he's having quite a time on those high heels!"

Far ahead, slipping and sliding in the lightly packed snow, Dan Mangan, carrying a load of schoolbooks, was making his way unsteadily among the trees.

Impulsively, Honey started up her horse and rode to the boy in the black leather jacket. Trixie hesitated a moment and then followed, wondering what Honey was up to.

Dan Mangan heard the sound of Starlight's hoofs and looked back, startled. When he saw who was coming, he scowled and stepped back off the path to let them go by.

But Honey pulled in a few feet away from him. "How about a lift? Those boots are too slippery for snow!" she laughed. "Climb on behind. We're on our way to see Mr. Maypenny."

Trixie stopped Susie a few feet behind Honey's horse and sat silent, staring at the dark-faced boy.

Dan Mangan scowled at them both. "I can make it okay. I don't need a lift."

"But there's no need of your walking when we're going to the same place," Honey said gently. "If you'd rather ride alone, Trix and I can double up and you can take Starlight, here. He's very gentle."

"I told you I don't want to ride," he said loudly, his scowl deepening. "You can't give me orders, even if I *do* work for your pa."

Honey's pretty face flushed and her eyes showed that she was hurt. She was gathering up her reins to ride on without answering, when Trixie spoke angrily.

"If you ask me, Hon, he just doesn't dare try to ride. He's afraid!" Trix didn't really mean it, but she had to say something unkind to punish the boy for hurting Honey's feelings.

"Oh, yeah?" Dan's lip curled. "Big talk, freckles. Climb down and I'll show you." He put his books down on a rock.

"Okay!" Trixie was out of the saddle in a flash. "Be sure you know which side to get on. Susie's particular."

She handed over the reins as Dan Mangan swaggered up beside Susie.

Susie's ears went back as Dan swung on, and she snorted. Trixie stepped back at once. "Take it easy, cowboy," she advised. "Maybe you'd better lengthen the stirrups. I keep them pretty short."

"Who's riding?" Dan answered shortly, and as he spoke he slapped the reins against Susie's neck. "Come on, move!"

Susie moved promptly. She kicked up her heels and

bucked. And then, ignoring Dan's attempt to hold her in, she made a dash for a stand of spruce close to the trail. "Stop her!" Honey called excitedly.

But it was too late. Susie had run under a low-hanging limb and unseated her rider. Dan Mangan went heels over head into the brush beside the trail, and the horrified girls saw him land hard and lie face down in the snow.

Chapter 8
The Black Leather Jacket

For a moment after the accident, the girls were too horrified to do anything but stare at Dan Mangan's limp body as he lay sprawled in the snow patch beside the bridle path.

Then Trixie, swallowing hard and trying to sound very brave, told Honey, "You go catch Susie before she runs too far, while I see if Dan's hurt."

Honey started after the mare, but she didn't have to go far. After brushing Dan off against the low-hanging tree limb, the saucy little mare had trotted only a few feet away into the brush, and was now browsing peacefully.

Trixie went up to Dan slowly, hoping hard that he wasn't badly hurt. She had had a course in first aid at school, but everything she had been taught was jumbled up in her mind now that she was facing a real crisis.

Then, as she knelt beside him, she was relieved to see Honey hurrying to join her. Maybe Honey could help with a suggestion, even though she had had no training that Trixie knew of.

"Dan! Dan Mangan!" Honey knelt on the other side of Dan. He was lying very still, apparently unconscious. "Maybe if we turned him over—" she whispered.

Trixie shook her head. "Better not. I've heard it's best never to move an accident victim till you're sure you won't do him worse harm by disturbing him. But we can't leave him here!"

Honey agreed hastily. "Maybe one of us should sit here by him, while the other brings Mr. Maypenny."

"Guess you're right," Trixie said uneasily. But before they could talk over which would go and which would stand by, the victim moaned and stirred. He rolled over onto his back suddenly and tried to sit up, only to fall back and hold his head. A large lump on the front of his forehead showed where he had landed on the hard ground.

Trixie gave a big sigh of relief. "Guess there's nothing broken after all," she told Honey.

Dan snatched his hands from his face and stared at the two girls with an unfriendly scowl. They both noticed a long tear in the sleeve of his black jacket. But aside from the bump and the torn sleeve, he seemed to be unhurt.

"Hi! How do you feel?" Honey asked quickly.

Dan touched the bump on his head and winced. "What happened?"

"Susie brushed you off on a tree limb," Honey explained. "I hope you aren't hurt?"

"Nah!" Dan scrambled unsteadily to his feet and stood swaying. "I'm okay." He even tried to smile at Honey.

"You don't look it," Trixie stated frankly. "You should have lengthened those stirrups and you would have had better control of Susie. I guess you don't know very much about riding." She didn't mean to sound smug, but that was how it sounded, even to her own ears.

Dan Mangan glared at her. "But *you* know all the answers, don't you, freckles?"

Trixie bit back a retort. She knew she deserved the reproof. She was sorry she had spoken that way.

"And now I suppose you'll run and tell old Maypenny I tried to break your horse's leg or something!" Dan sneered, his dark eyes angry.

"I will not!" Trixie was getting angry. "And you ought to be ashamed to speak about your grandfather so disrespectfully!"

"My which? Haw! That old square from squaresville?" Dan laughed harshly. "He's no relation of mine, and quit saying so!" He was brushing the snow from his clothes as he spoke, but they both noticed that when he felt the tear in his jacket sleeve he looked worried and fingered it uncertainly, pulling the two edges of the tear together.

Honey spoke hurriedly and with a friendly smile. "If you'd like, I can mend that for you so it won't even show. I'll get a needle and black thread from Mr. Maypenny."

For a moment, Dan looked as if he intended to accept Honey's friendly offer. Then he glanced at Trixie and saw her staring critically at him. He flushed and told Honey with a frown, "Don't bother. I don't need anybody's help."

Honey drew back as if she had been slapped. It made Trixie furious. "You could at least say thanks!" she told him bitingly. "You're just lucky if Honey doesn't tell Mr. Maypenny that you tried to ride one of her horses and you didn't know how and it was a wonder you didn't break its neck!" She had to stop for breath.

"Go on, tell him!" Dan turned to Honey. "And you can tell your rich pa, too, while you're at it! I won't be stuck in this hick town long enough for it to make any difference to me!" And with that, Dan Mangan picked up his books and strode off up the bridle path.

The two girls stared after him. He slipped and slid a bit on the snowy ground, but he stayed on his feet till he went out of sight among the trees.

"He makes me want to chew nails!" Trixie stormed.

But Honey looked troubled. "Did you notice how sad he looked when he saw that tear in his jacket?"

"No, I didn't," Trixie snapped. "He looks just plain mean to *me,* all the time!"

"Or scared, maybe," Honey guessed.

Trixie's eyes widened. "Hey, maybe it's horses he's afraid of. He doesn't want anybody to know it, and that's why he pretended he knew how to ride!"

"That's it, of course!" Honey agreed quickly. "And he got angry with you because you guessed it!"

Trixie nodded gravely. "It's too bad he has to leave soon. We could get Regan to teach him. I bet he'd get over being afraid of horses once he learned to ride."

"And if we don't start riding again pretty soon," Honey reminded her, "we never will get to Mr. Maypenny's to look at his almanac."

"Come on, then," Trixie laughed. "But don't go offering Mr. Dan Mangan a lift when we catch up with him. We'll just ride right along without him."

But they never did catch up with Dan Mangan that day. For a half mile or so they rode abreast along the bridle path and then went single file as it narrowed. Trixie, riding ahead, studied the imprints of Dan's boots in the snow, until suddenly they disappeared on a rocky stretch in the shelter of an ancient evergreen. She knew that he had struck out from the trail, probably on a short cut or to look at the jack rabbit snares Mr. Maypenny always set at the boundaries of his property to keep "varmints" out of his winter vegetable patch.

There was no sign of the boy at Mr. Maypenny's, and they decided not to say anything about the accident. Mr. Maypenny seemed glad to see them and offered them hot chocolate if they wanted it.

"No, thanks, Mr. Maypenny." Honey smiled at him. "We're late, and we'll have to start right back."

"That's too bad, youngsters. I was hoping you could stay a little and visit with the boy Danny. He says he's met you all at school."

"That's right," Trixie nodded. "Will he be here long?"

"Rest of the term, I hope. The boy's a help already, even though he's innocent as a babe about farm life." He interrupted himself abruptly. "But here I am gabbling, when you're wanting to look at the almanac. Here it is, hanging right by the stove, where I can look at it every morning and know what to expect outdoors!"

"We thought the twenty-seventh would be about right, on a Saturday—" Trixie was thumbing over the pages. "Here! 'Clear and cold.' That's elegant! I hope your almanac's telling the truth!"

"Hasn't missed yet!" Mr. Maypenny asserted. Then he looked a little sheepish and corrected himself, "That is, all except the hurricane last November. Book said 'fair weather' that time."

"Oh, well." Trixie held back a grin. "Anybody can make *one* mistake, 'specially a small one!"

But as she and Honey rode back toward Glen Road a few minutes later, they had a good laugh about the almanac and the hurricane.

There was a little scraped place on the mare Susie's flank and the girls had to explain to Regan how it had happened.

His face darkened as they told him about Dan Mangan's accident with Susie. "He must learn to keep off the horses," he said grimly when Trixie had finished.

"I bet he won't try again," Trixie laughed.

"But he should," Honey argued. "Mr. Maypenny says he hopes Dan will stay till summer vacation. And it would make things lots easier for Mr. Maypenny if his helper could ride. He could cover lots more ground."

"So he could," Regan agreed heartily. "Maybe we can spare old Spartan for the lad to use. I don't get him out as often as I should. I'll speak to Miss Trask about it

next time I see her." Regan beamed at them.

Trixie thought, watching him, *He certainly looks a lot happier than he did before he went to the city about his experiment, whatever it is. Maybe it's working out so he'll be rich and famous.*

Regan was telling Honey, "Tell the boys I'll be glad to lend them a hand building the booths for the carnival."

"They'll be glad to hear that," Trixie grinned, "but you better tell them yourself. They'd think I begged you to help, so I could get out of some of the work."

Regan chuckled. He seemed in high good spirits. "Don't worry! I'll put 'em straight. I might even swing in Maypenny and the Mangan boy for good measure! They'll be glad to do what they can, too."

Trixie remembered suddenly. "But Dan told us he was leaving very soon. Remember, Honey?"

Honey nodded. "I'd forgotten that."

Regan's face was stern. "He did, eh?" He was silent a moment, as if he were thinking it over. Then he said abruptly, "Well, run along to the farm, girls. I'll take care of the horses and the tack today. I'm caught up on all the rest of my work."

"Jeeps! Thanks a lot, Regan. We *are* late, and Moms has choir practice tonight, too!" Trixie grabbed Honey's hand and drew her out of the barn with her. "Let's scoot!"

But once they were on their way down the driveway, they didn't hurry a great deal. Trixie had something on her mind that was bothering her, and Honey noticed it after a couple of her own remarks got grunts for an answer.

Honey stopped suddenly and faced her friend. "All right. What is it now? What are you wondering about this time?"

Trixie looked serious. "You know, Honey, it's a funny thing. Remember I thought Dan looked like somebody I knew but I couldn't think who it was? I know now."

"Goodness! *Who?*"

"Regan!"

"Oh, Trix! That's silly. Regan has red hair and Dan is very dark."

"I know, but just the same, there's something around their eyes that's the same."

"Well, I can't see that. *I* think Dan Mangan looks more like Mr. Maypenny. They have the same sharp, stuck-out chin."

Trixie looked startled. "I didn't notice that, but they do have, don't they? That's funny. I guess maybe our hunch that Dan is Mr. Maypenny's grandson makes more sense than thinking Regan's related to him, at that." She seemed disappointed.

"I think so," Honey agreed, "no matter *what* Dan says."

"Oh, dear," Trixie sighed. "I thought I had a brand-new mystery." She clutched Honey's arm suddenly and pointed down the drive toward the cottage clubhouse. "Hey, the door's open! Wonder who's in there."

"Let's find out!" Honey answered, and they ran down the driveway toward the cottage. "I hope Jim's home!"

But when they went inside, there was no one in the pretty little "conference" room with its table and chairs. The posters were spread out on the table and the paints were unopened, just as the boys had left them to wait for Jim to come back from the field trip to the Catskills.

Honey poked her head around the end of the plywood partition that closed off the storage area where their summer and winter sports equipment was neatly stacked. It was darker in there. "Nobody here!" she called out.

A moment later, she gave a shriek and came backing away. "An animal! I saw some kind of a wild animal in there!" She grabbed Trixie and pulled her toward the front door. "Come on, let's get out of here!"

"What kind of an animal?" Trixie's curiosity was stronger than her fears. She took a step toward the partition, but Honey held on to her arm.

"Don't go! It was big and fuzzy and has beady eyes!" Her teeth were chattering. "I'm sure it's a bear!"

Chapter 9
Jim's Advice

"A bear?" Trixie grabbed Honey's hand. "Let's get out of here!"

They ran for the door, sure that the bear was close on their heels. But when they were safely outside the cottage clubhouse, and dared to look back, there was no sign of the bear. The doorway was empty.

"Thank goodness! He probably was as scared of me as I was of him!" Honey giggled nervously. "Now what do we do to get rid of him?"

"Get rid of whom?" Jim's voice came as a surprise.

He was standing behind them, several cardboard posters tucked under his arm, and a grin on his face.

"Oh, Jim! I'm so glad you got back! There's a horrible big bear in our clubhouse! What can we do to chase him out?" Honey asked, a little hysterically.

"A bear? In there?" Jim didn't seem too worried.

"I'd better call Regan," Trixie suggested hastily.

"No need," Jim assured her confidently. "It's probably only a cub and I can handle it. Just wait here."

"But it looked big to me!" Honey protested. "Please don't get hurt, Jim."

"No chance," he boasted and strode bravely toward the doorway.

"Here, grab this and let's help." Trixie was handing Honey a length of firewood from the pile against the toolshed and taking a second for herself.

"Hit him on the nose, if you get a chance," Trixie instructed Honey. "It's their most vulner—" She bogged down uncertainly on the long word. "I mean, it hurts beasts the most to be hit on the nose!"

"I should think so," Honey shuddered.

Up ahead, Jim disappeared into the clubhouse, and for a moment the two girls held back, listening fearfully. There was no sound of a struggle inside the cottage.

"Maybe it went back to sleep when we went away," Trixie whispered hopefully, edging nearer.

They got close enough to the doorway to peer inside, but it was too dark in there for them to see anything. And there wasn't a sound.

"I guess we'd better go on in. Jim may need us," Trixie told Honey under her breath.

They both wanted to run away, but they went through the open doorway, and there on the conference table was a bear, black and fuzzy and staring at them with shiny eyes. But it wasn't a live bear. It was standing on a platform with rollers, and it was wearing a pretty red leather harness.

Jim was grinning at them from the other side of the room. "Meet Mister Bear!" he laughed.

"Jim! It's darling!" They made a rush for it. "Where did it come from?" Honey asked.

"We dragged it home from Sleepyside," Mart's voice came from the doorway. "The toy-shop man, Mr. Martin, donated it as a prize for the best skater under ten years old at the carnival!" Mart and Brian were coming in with their arms loaded with stuff. "Wait till you see all the loot we picked up! Everybody thinks our carnival is a great idea. We practically sold all the space in the program!"

"And we have the principal's permission to use the printing press at school to run the programs off!" Brian added proudly.

"I hope you informed this bear trainer that he's supposed to do the posters!" Trixie wrinkled her nose at Jim. She hadn't forgiven him for fooling her and Honey.

Jim grinned at her. "They gave me all the bad news, and I'll start working right after school tomorrow, Madame President."

"What about the lumber company?" Honey asked as they unwrapped some of the prizes.

"We asked for the flooring, and it looks like we'll get it. How's that?" Mart gloated.

"Perfect! Everything's perfect!" Trixie said dreamily.

"Except Moms was looking for you when we stopped by there just now," Brian told her drily.

"Yeeks! I forgot again!" Trixie dashed for the door.

"Wait for me!" Honey laughed, and a moment later they were running down the driveway, headed for the Belden farm.

The telephone was ringing in the kitchen when they came dashing in. Mrs. Belden, looking very harassed, was trying to peel potatoes and keep Bobby out of the cooky jar at the same time.

"I'll talk to you later!" she told Trixie. "Take over with Bobby. Get him ready for dinner. And, Honey, look at the roast, please." She dashed for the phone.

The girls obeyed the orders quickly, but as Trixie was leading Bobby upstairs for a wash-up, she heard her mother say, "Why, yes, Miss Trask. I think it's a splendid idea. It might help a lot."

A few minutes later when Honey joined her to help with Bobby and wash her own hands and face, she was full of curiosity about the conversation. "Did

Moms tell you what Miss Trask's splendid idea was?"

"Goodness, you hear everything!" Honey teased her. Then she sobered. "It was about Dan Mangan. She's given Regan permission to lend old Spartan to Mr. Maypenny so Dan can do his patrolling in the game preserve on horseback."

"I suppose Miss Trask wants us to teach him how to ride!" Trixie frowned.

"I don't mind. I'll be glad to. We can talk to him about it tomorrow morning while we're all waiting for the bus."

But Dan Mangan didn't take that bus to school. He had gone in earlier. And all that week he went in earlier than they did, and when he met any of them on the school grounds, he either pretended not to see them, or he answered their greetings as briefly as possible.

At lunch on Friday, he sat with a group of boys a couple of tables away from the Bob-Whites, and he seemed to be very popular with them as he swaggered and sprawled at the table and talked big about his life in the city.

"Listen to him!" Trixie whispered darkly to Jim. "That story he's telling about how he talked back to the police captain when he was arrested! I bet he never *was* arrested in his whole life! And if he was, I bet he was too scared to peep!" She laughed, but Jim didn't laugh with her.

Instead, Jim looked serious. The others were busy talking over details of the carnival plans with Di Lynch, and Jim took the opportunity to speak soberly to Trixie.

"I don't know why Dan Mangan's out in the country here working for Mr. Maypenny, but I get the idea somehow that he isn't here because he wants to be. And I can tell by the look in his eyes that no matter how big he talks, he's scared."

Trixie frowned. "That's sort of funny, Jim. You know, Honey said almost the same thing. She thought he looked sad, too. But I think he just looks ornery."

"I know somebody else who had the same reputation not so long ago. He was a runaway kid that didn't believe anybody'd want to be friends with him. Then he met two girls who made him change his mind. They even helped give him a sister and a dad and mother he's very fond of."

Trixie looked at him solemnly a moment. "You mean *you*. And thanks for saying nice things about Honey and me. But it isn't fair for you to say you were like Dan Mangan. You didn't wear a black leather jacket and silly cowboy boots and talk about what a big man you were someplace else!"

Jim's eyes twinkled. "There's nothing wrong with a black leather jacket, Trix. It's warm. And it's probably all Dan Mangan has to wear."

Trixie looked troubled. "I guess maybe you're right, Jim."

"Try to be nice to the kid, Trix, even if it hurts you. You might be surprised. He could turn out to be quite a regular guy, once he gets used to being away from home and decides to make new friends."

"Well, I'll try," Trixie promised, but she wasn't very sure of herself.

She told Honey what Jim had said, as they rode out the next afternoon on Susie and Starlight toward the game preserve. Mrs. Belden was sending some of her canned fruit to Mr. Maypenny. The old gamekeeper was very fond of spiced crabapples, but there wasn't a crabapple tree on his property.

"So I'm waving a flag of truce at the enemy," Trixie said airily. "I may get shot, but I'll be doing my best to make peace."

Honey nodded. "Good for you!" and a moment later, as she glanced ahead and a little to one side of the trail, she reined in and said, "Get out your white flag, Trix. The enemy has been sighted. Look up there on that hill in that clump of oaks."

Trixie stopped Susie and squinted at the distant trees. "I don't see—yes, there he is!" She cupped her hands around her mouth and called, "Yoo-hoo, Dan! We've got something for you!" She waved a friendly hand.

But the slim figure in the black jacket and shiny-peaked cap disappeared among the oaks without showing any sign that he had heard Trixie calling him.

"The flag of truce just came down with a dull thud," Trixie said grimly. "He doesn't want to be chummy."

They rode on, and when they were in sight of Mr. Maypenny's sturdy little cabin, they heard the sound of hammering. The sound was coming from the barn behind the cabin, where Mr. Maypenny kept Brownie.

"Let's show him what we've brought for him," Trixie suggested. "I love to see his face light up when he sees good food. Maybe he'll be so happy he'll make us some hot chocolate with cinnamon in it."

They dismounted a few yards from the barn and tied their horses to a post. Trixie took the jar with the pinkest of the crabapples floating enticingly in syrup, and they went toward the barn.

The hammering was still going on as they stepped in out of the wintry sunlight. They saw that a new stall was being built, and that Spartan's name had already been lettered on a rough-finished board above it.

But the whistler, who broke off his merry tune and straightened up at the sight of them, was not Mr. Maypenny. It was Dan Mangan, in his shirtsleeves.

"Maypenny ain't here. He's out checking the feeding stations," Dan said shortly, unsmiling.

"Oh." Trixie was doing her best to be bright and friendly. "We thought that was you we saw out there a few minutes ago in the oak grove."

Dan shook his head. "I don't know what you're talking about. I've been right around here ever since I got home from school last night."

Trixie frowned. "It didn't look like Mr. Maypenny."

"Meaning you think I'm lying?" he asked curtly.

"Trixie didn't mean any such thing," Honey said in quick defense of her friend. "She meant that whoever it was that we saw was wearing a black jacket and cap. We know that Mr. Maypenny always wears a turtleneck sweater and funny-looking wool knickers and a red cap and looks quaint."

"You saw somebody wearing a black jacket and a cap?" Dan asked, suddenly serious.

"Of course we did," Trixie said impatiently. "And you saw *us,* too. You were looking right at us when we

waved. And I don't know why you're trying to say it wasn't you."

"Because it wasn't!" Dan's black eyes snapped with anger. "Either it was old Maypenny you saw or some tramp."

"Hey, maybe it was a tramp, Honey!" Trixie hadn't thought of that possibility before. "He didn't want us to see him, so he ducked."

"I suppose it could have been," Honey agreed, "unless Mr. Maypenny has borrowed your jacket and cap."

"Nope," Dan said flatly. He cocked his thumb toward the wall of the other stall where old Spartan was calmly munching on oats and ignoring them. "There's my stuff." He laughed suddenly. "You two better get yourselves some eyeglasses. You've been seeing things."

"But—" Trixie flushed angrily at his tone of voice. She wasn't used to being sneered at. When Mart teased her, it was always in fun. This dark-haired boy seemed to mean it, and it hurt.

Honey laid a hand on Trixie's arm and stopped her from making an angry reply. "Let's leave the fruit at the house. We'll be late getting home, and your mother will have a fit." She drew Trixie away before there could be any more argument.

"I still don't understand it," Trixie said crossly as

they rode home along the trail a few minutes later.

"I suppose it's simple enough," Honey sighed. "We saw Mr. Maypenny up in the oak grove. And it was so shadowy up among those trees that we both made a mistake about what he was wearing. Those snow patches are so bright up there when the sun hits them that it probably dazzled our eyes."

"Maybe, but I still don't believe it," Trixie insisted stubbornly. "Look up there, on top of that rock—up ahead. That must be over fifty yards away, and I can see a baby squirrel sitting there just as plain as if he were only ten feet from us. Well, if we can see things that far away when the woods are shadowier than they were half an hour ago, why, we must have seen whoever was in the oak grove a great deal clearer. And I still say it was Dan Mangan, no matter what *he* says. He's the only person around Sleepyside who wears a black leather jacket and a funny black cap!"

"But why is he being so stubborn about admitting it?" Honey puzzled.

"I think I know!" Trixie's blue eyes sparkled. "I bet Mr. Maypenny told him not to leave the yard and he's been out prowling around in the woods instead. He was afraid that you and I might tell Mr. Maypenny on him if he owned up to it!"

"You could be right," Honey agreed, looking relieved. "In fact, the more I think about it, the more I'm sure you are. It's too bad."

"What is?" Trixie was surprised.

"That Dan thinks we would have tattled. All he would have had to do was to ask us not to say anything about seeing him out there, and we wouldn't have."

Trixie looked uncomfortable. "I guess it's my fault," she sighed. "I try to be nice to him, but—well, he just sort of rubs me the wrong way, Honey. You know, they say if you rub a cat's fur the wrong way, it sends out sparks. That's me, shooting out sparks. And I can't seem to stop."

Chapter 10
The Big Cat

The two girls rode in silence for a few minutes, guiding the horses carefully down the narrow, rocky trail that was still bordered with patches of snow.

Here and there, where some of the snow had melted, it was slippery going for the horses and they were well splashed with mud.

"Boy! Will we have a messy job cleaning up these animals!" Trixie grumbled. "Why does the snow have to melt into nasty old mud? The only person that likes mud is Bobby. I think he likes the taste of it—"

Trixie broke off suddenly as something in the patch of snow close to her drew her attention. She reined in and Honey, coming close behind on Starlight, had to stop suddenly to avoid bumping into her.

Trixie leaned down from her saddle and studied some marks in the snow. "Look at this. What kind of animal do you suppose left these tracks?"

Honey tried to look past Starlight's head, but it was hard to do. "What do they look like? You're my big brother Jim's star pupil when it comes to wildlife."

"His dumbest, you mean," Trixie corrected her with a grin. "I'm the one who got all excited about seeing a wolf track a couple of weeks ago, and it turned out to be Reddy's!" Reddy was the Beldens' wholly untrained but lovable red setter.

"I remember!" Honey smiled. "We had a lot of fun about it."

"These aren't wolf or Reddy tracks, though. These were made by an animal of the cat family. I see the thick pad marks." Trixie swung out of her saddle to examine them.

Honey hesitated a moment and then dismounted. She looped her reins over her wrist as she led Starlight closer and bent to study the tracks.

Trixie pointed. "See the claw marks there."

"Claw marks? Ugh!" Honey stared at the tracks. "Trix, if a cat has feet and claws that big, it's a lot bigger cat than I want to meet! Let's get out of here!"

"Oh, pooh! It's probably just a wildcat. They aren't much bigger than Mr. Lytell's big ol' tomcat, but they do have bigger feet, I guess."

"Wildcat?" Honey glanced around apprehensively. "Here?"

"Jim says there are wildcats up in the highest peaks of the Catskills. But they don't come down this low very often. And there even are catamounts."

"Catamounts? You mean those big mountain lions?" Honey's eyes were pools of alarm. "What are they doing here?"

"Just living on littler animals, I guess. Jim says this whole valley used to be full of bears and catamounts and bison. The settlers had plenty of trouble with them."

"But, suppose a wildcat *did* leave those tracks. Wouldn't it be a good idea to go before he decides to make a meal of us?" Honey shivered.

Trixie chuckled. "Jim says they're afraid of people. They'd never attack a man unless they were practically starving and he looked tasty." She grinned at Honey. "I don't know what they'd think of *us.*"

"Ugh! Don't talk like that!" Honey knew Trixie was only joking, but she didn't relish the thought of being on a wildcat's dinner menu. "Do you think we ought to ride back and tell Mr. Maypenny about seeing these tracks? He'll want to hunt down the creature before it slaughters any of our darling deer!"

Trixie got to her feet suddenly. "Honey! You know what I think? I bet Mr. Maypenny is out hunting this wildcat, right now. That's why he wasn't at the cabin! I thought there was something funny about his being out checking the feeding stations this late in the day. He probably told Dan to tell us that, in case we came by, so we wouldn't worry if we heard he was tracking a wildcat!"

Honey nodded, but she looked around uneasily. "Maybe it's still around somewhere close. We'd better go."

"Pooh! Don't worry! Jim says they hunt only at night. It's probably asleep in a nice warm cave somewhere right now."

The words were hardly out of her mouth before a weird, hoarse cry came from somewhere on the side of the mountain only a few hundred yards away.

Instantly, the two horses panicked, and while the yowl echoed and re-echoed through the woods, they fought to get away. Snorting loudly, Starlight tried to free himself from the reins still wrapped around Honey's wrist. Honey struggled to control him, slipping and sliding on the rocky, muddy ground of the trail.

Susie reared and pawed the air, whinnying with fright. Trixie had to retreat or be hit by the flailing hoofs of her usually gentle mount. The moment that Trixie was out of the way, Susie came down on all fours and ran down the trail. "Come back here, you silly!" Trixie shouted. "Whoa, Susie! Good girl! Whoa!" She plunged down the trail after the runaway.

There was no telling when she would have caught up with the terrified horse, except that Susie's dangling reins caught in a crevice between two rocks along the trail and halted her with a violent jerk. It pulled her almost off her feet and left her so confused and frightened that Trixie had very little trouble, a moment later, taking control of her. Step by step, Trixie led her back up the trail to where Honey was just getting Starlight calmed.

Both horses were trembling so violently and were so skittish that the girls had difficulty remounting. Once they were in their saddles again and had started Starlight and Susie homeward, they never slackened their pace till they were safely out on Glen Road.

"That cat thing was practically on our n-n-necks," Trixie shuddered as they turned in at the Wheeler driveway. "I think maybe Starlight and Susie could smell it, whatever it was."

It was almost dark by the time they had groomed the horses and taken care of the tack. They noticed that the rest of the horses had been attended to and fed, but there was no sign of any of the boys or of Regan.

"I'm almost scared to walk home," Trixie said as they started out with their flashlights. "I know I'll be feeling big yellow cat's eyes watching every step and switching their tails ready to pounce!"

"Cat's eyes with tails?" Mart called out from the bench at the bus stop. "Where do you get those?"

At the sound of his voice, each girl gave a little shriek of surprise, but a moment later they were telling him breathlessly about the wildcat they had almost met.

"Huh!" Mart got up and fell into step with them, holding an arm of each. "That's one of the best excuses for being late, Miss Alibi, that you've ever thought up! Congratulations!"

"I'm afraid Moms won't think much of it, even if it *is* true!" Trixie moaned. "I can see the fire in her eye from here!"

"Surprise!" Mart grinned. "Dad and Moms went to White Plains on a shopping expedition, and Jim and Brian are whipping up a delectable repast of hot dogs and hamburgers for us all. So no scolding tonight!"

"Thank goodness!" Trixie said fervently. "After all we've been through, I just know I wouldn't have been able to live another minute if Moms had so much as frowned at me!"

"And now that my moron sister is back to normal, suppose you let me tell you that Jim has finished sketching the posters, and tomorrow you artists start filling in the colors, pr-ronto! So Brian and I will be able to distribute them to the worthy merchants who have promised their support—to say nothing of the prizes we're hoping they'll donate, one and all!"

"We'll get at them first thing in the morning!" Trixie promised happily. "Where are the posters now?"

"At the banquet hall—I mean, our kitchen."

They were turning in at the gate of Crabapple Farm just then, laughing and talking excitedly, when Jim appeared on the front porch and rang the old-fashioned dinner gong.

"Coming, son!" Mart shouted, and they all trooped up onto the porch and into the house.

The boys had set the kitchen table for the meal, and Bobby had been enthroned at one end, well out of the line of traffic. His eyes were big with excitement, and he yelled, "Hi, Trixie and Honey! Look at me!" to the girls as they entered. "I'm hungry!"

"Don't rush the cook, buddy!" Brian warned as he stood over the stove in a haze of smoke from well-sizzled hamburgers. "And the rest of you, finish setting the table!"

There was so much excitement over the amateur cooking going on, and so much confusion for the next few minutes, that the girls didn't tell their experiences in the woods. But when they finally all sat down to enjoy the scorched hamburgers, plus all the trimmings that Mrs. Belden had left perfectly prepared for their dinner, Trixie announced, "You're just lucky we ever got here tonight," in her most dramatic tones.

"Now that sounds like a cue line," Brian told her gravely. "Am I supposed to ask you to go on?"

"Just try and stop her!" Mart snickered.

But when Trixie, with Honey's excited help, had told about the wildcat tracks and the horrible howling that had panicked their horses, Jim didn't laugh or try to joke about it.

"Just how big were the tracks?" he asked Trixie seriously. "And about how far apart were they?"

And when the girls had agreed on the size of the tracks and measured off along the table edge just about how great the distance had been between them, Jim nodded grimly. "It sounds to me as if you missed meeting a lot bigger animal than a mere wildcat!"

"Catamount?" Brian asked quickly.

Jim nodded, his expression serious. "Possibly. And from the length of its stride, if the girls remember rightly, it was a grand-daddy of its species!"

"No wonder those poor horses were hysterical!" Trixie shivered. "I hope Mr. Maypenny—er—catches up with it." She glanced at Bobby as she hastily substituted the word "catches" for "kills," the word she had started to say.

Jim noticed her glance and nodded reassuringly. "Oh, I imagine he will. He has quite a reputation in Sleepyside as a—uh—catamount catcher."

"I wanna go see the kitty. Trixie said we could have another kitty. Maybe I can have this one. Huh, Trixie?" Bobby's eyes reflected his excitement. "I hope it has spots."

"I'm afraid not, Bobby," Brian spoke quickly. "Not this kind of a kitty. It's a dirty-looking tan color, and—"

"And it has long, sharp claws!" Trixie concluded for him.

"Oh!" Bobby wrinkled his nose. "I guess I don't want it."

Mart said, "Next spring, you and I will go looking together for a cute little kitty that you can cuddle. I think I know where there'll be a whole family of them, in Mr. Maypenny's barn. And you can pick out the one you want. How's that, skipper?"

"You'll forget." Bobby's eyes were misty and his lower lip began to tremble, a sure sign of tears on the way.

"Cross my heart an' hope to die," his big brother

promised solemnly and went through the necessary motions.

"Now eat the rest of your dinner, and I'll read you two whole stories at bedtime, any two you want to hear—how's that?" Honey asked him gaily.

"Okay!" Sunshine broke through the clouds, and Bobby went back contentedly to the rest of his slightly charred but tasty hamburger sandwich, while the carefully guarded talk went on around him. There was a strict rule in the Belden household that Bobby was not to be terrified by fearsome stories at any time, and least of all just before bedtime. His imagination was a little too strong sometimes, as it was.

Jim spoke casually. "I think Brian and I will ride out that way tomorrow, or Monday before school. I want to see those tracks if they're still there. I may measure and sketch them for a paper I'm doing on the carnivores of our valley."

"Good idea," Brian agreed, "and meanwhile, you girls stick around home for a change. We'll exercise your horses for you, while you get busy coloring those posters. Jim's managed to get some terrific ideas in them and we're anxious to have a few painted and ready to place around town where our book-donating customers can see them."

"We'll get right on them," Trixie assured him. She was just as eager to have the posters finished as the boys were. She and Honey had written Dolores and Lupe about the ice carnival benefit they were planning, and she wanted to be able to tell them in her next letter that things were shaping up just fine.

All three of the boys drifted over to talk to Regan after dinner. And for once, Trixie didn't mind not having them help with the dishes. She was tired, and she didn't think she could stand any of Mart's teasing tonight.

Honey had trotted Bobby up to bed as soon as the boys had left, and was probably, Trixie thought wearily, in the middle of the second of those all-too-familiar stories by this time. Honey was a real friend, and Trixie decided she wouldn't know how to get along without her now.

The hallway door swung open with a bang, and Honey, her big hazel eyes wide with alarm, rushed in. "Trixie!"

Trixie almost dropped the dish she was washing.

"What's happened? Bobby?"

"No." Honey sank onto the nearest chair and pushed up her left sweater sleeve to show her bare wrist. "My watch! It's gone!"

Chapter 11
More Suspicions

"Oh, is that all?" Trixie was weak with relief that there was nothing the matter with Bobby. "You probably forgot to put it on this morning."

Honey shook her head, big tears starting to fill her eyes. "No, I remember, this morning when I was dressing I took it out of my leather jewel box just to look at it—"

Trixie interrupted. "I didn't know you kept it there. I thought you hung it on that ceramic jewelry-tree where I put mine every night when I take it off."

Honey nodded. "I do. *That* watch, my everyday one. This was the one Mother gave me that *her* mother gave *her* when she finished school. My dress-up watch."

"You wore that one to go riding?" Trixie was frankly shocked. "What on earth for?"

"I don't know. I just thought, 'It's so pretty. I'll wear it today and enjoy it!' " She burst into sobs. "What am I going to do?"

"Stop crying first," Trixie advised, patting her shoulder, "and maybe we can think of something. I'm sure it can't be very far away. Let's start thinking."

They had been many places and done many things that day. The stables, the clubhouse—it was going to be hard to decide where to begin looking.

"Let's see, now. Where could you have loosened it accidentally and not noticed?"

"Oh, I don't know!" Honey had almost dried her tears but they started to flow again. "It had such a good strong catch on it. It was hard to open. I always had to pull a lot on it before I could get it unfastened. Mother said that the catch was made like that because the watch was so valuable!"

"Mmmm." Trixie was thinking. "Let's see, now. If something pulled on your wrist—hey, wait a sec! Remember how you kept hold of the reins when you dismounted to look at those cat tracks? Which hand did you use?"

"Why, I looped the reins over my wrist—this one," Honey touched her bare left wrist, "naturally."

"Don't you see?" Trixie was excited. "Starlight tried to pull loose and the reins must have sprung open the catch on your watch band!"

"Trixie! My watch is probably lying out there in the woods right now!"

"Well, it could be," Trixie admitted with a grin.

"So let's start looking there tomorrow morning."

"Wonderful!" Honey beamed. Then, just as suddenly, she looked worried. "Only—Brian said we shouldn't ride."

"That's mostly because he thinks we're afraid of the cat! But the thing's probably miles and miles away by now, or it will be by morning."

"Or else Mr. Maypenny may have shot it," Honey suggested eagerly.

"We'll have to get the horses out before the boys are stirring. Are you game?" Trixie asked. "Of course, if we run into Regan, he may forbid us to go."

"We don't have to tell him which way we are riding, do we?" Honey's eyes sparkled.

"Of course not! We can start off as if we were merely going to the crossroads to see Mr. Lytell at his store, and then cut across to the road to the preserve."

And that's just what they did early the next morning.

They tiptoed down to the kitchen in the early dawn of the winter day, snatched a glass of milk apiece and a cold biscuit to sustain them till breakfast, and then stole out by way of the kitchen door.

Mrs. Belden, going quietly into Bobby's room to see if he was covered, saw them going down the path to the gate, still unconsciously tiptoeing. *Now what are those two up to?* she smiled to herself. *Probably hurrying over to the clubhouse to light the stove so it will be comfortable to paint there today.*

The sun was just coming up as the girls walked their horses out of the Wheeler stables and down the driveway. The frosty air nipped their ears and reddened the tips of their noses, but they took long deep breaths as they trudged along leading their favorites, Starlight and Susie.

Once they were past the clubhouse and out of range of the driveway and the garage at the head of it, they mounted and trotted the two horses along the road toward the turn-off that led up into the game preserve.

It was very quiet along Glen Road. Sleepyside traffic started late on Sundays. The woods were even more quiet, and cold. The girls were both a little sorry that they had come out alone so early in the morning. It would have been lots more cheerful to have had the boys with them.

"How much farther is it to where we stopped?" Trixie asked. "Things look different when the shadows point the other way."

"It can't be more than half a mile, remember?"

Honey was trying to be cheerful. "We'll snatch up the watch and turn around and head for home."

"You bet!" Trixie agreed fervently.

A moment later, Susie stumbled on a loose rock and struggled to regain her footing. And when she went on, she limped a little on her left front hoof.

The moment Trixie noticed the limp, she stopped the little mare and dismounted. "I'd better see if she's picked up a pebble," she told Honey. "Won't take a minute."

"We're almost there anyhow," Honey answered cheerfully. "No rush." But she looked around her nervously and stared up toward the higher slopes on either side of the trail for signs of last evening's cat.

Trixie examined Susie's hoof. "Oops! There it is. A sharp-pointed, nasty little stone. Poor li'l Susie—I'll get it out right now." She used a small stick to pry out the offending pebble.

Honey sat erect suddenly in the saddle, her eyes wide. "Ssss!" she signaled to Trixie. "Listen!"

They both heard the crashing of brush somewhere beyond the turn of the trail. Somebody or something was coming. At first, they both thought it might be the big cat, but the sound of heavy boots striking against rocks told them the newcomer was human.

"It's probably Mr. Maypenny or Dan Mangan," Trixie said cheerfully. She spoke in her normal voice, expecting to see one of them turning the corner at any moment. Instead, the sound of the steps stopped. Dead silence followed.

Trixie and Honey looked at each other uneasily. "A poacher!" Honey said softly. "Let's give him time to get away. Dad says sometimes poachers get mean if they think a person has recognized them. We don't want to see him if we can help it."

So they waited a couple of minutes, but it was scary waiting. Not a sound came from up ahead.

"We can't just sit here," Trixie whispered tensely. "He's probably watching us. We'll have to pretend we don't care who it was and aren't suspicious. Let's just ride on."

"Okay." Honey was uneasy. "Come on."

Trixie mounted hastily and not too gracefully. A moment later, she was riding ahead up the trail toward the game preserve, with Honey close behind her on Starlight. She even pretended a careless whistle, but it wasn't very strong, and was quite off-key.

They were almost to the cross-trail where they had heard the cat's yowl, before they felt secure. Honey had looked back along the trail several times but had seen no one. With distance between themselves and the brush-crasher, they began to feel more relaxed.

"It was probably Dan Mangan, and he was still sulking at us," Honey said. "But he certainly didn't have to hide."

"I don't think it was Dan," Trixie looked solemn. "I just have a feeling it was a poacher."

"Well, here we are," Honey said as they came in sight of the cross-trail. "We'll find my watch and then ride back home as fast as we can. If we meet anyone and he tries to stop us, we'll ride right past in a hurry. He'll have to move out of the way if we don't hesitate!"

They dismounted hurriedly and tied the horses to a pair of birch saplings beside the trail.

"Here's where Starlight was cutting up," Honey said. "It's probably among these rocks. Oh, I hope it didn't get smashed!" She got down on her knees and started to search closely through the dried underbrush.

But Trixie, coming to help her, said suddenly, "Somebody else has been here. Look! Footprints all around on the snow patches!"

Honey stared at them a moment. "Not the boys'. None of them wear pointed cowboy boots with high heels."

"Dan Mangan!" Trixie exclaimed. "He's been here

and probably found your watch. That's a break!"

"I hope he found it before the wet snow got into it! Let's go get it and tomorrow I'll take it to the watch repairman in Sleepyside to be checked over. What luck!" Honey was radiant with relief. "What if some stranger had found it!"

"Or if it had fallen deep in the snow and hadn't been found till the snow melted!" Trixie added. "It might have rusted so badly it could never be fixed!"

They mounted again as quickly as possible and rode on cheerfully toward the Maypenny cabin.

Mr. Maypenny was busy in his little kitchen, and the smell of hot doughnuts frying in deep fat greeted them as he opened the door at their knock.

"Bless your hearts!" he chuckled. "I had no idea my visitors would be back again so soon. Will you sit down and have some fresh milk and hot cinnamon doughnuts?"

"Oh, boy!" Trixie's grin spread. Mr. Maypenny's doughnuts were almost as tasty as his venison stew. "I didn't know how hungry I was! We didn't have any breakfast."

Mr. Maypenny shook his head. "That's not like Mrs. Belden, letting you two ride out on a cold morning without something warm inside you."

"Moms didn't know we were up, much less riding," Trixie confided. "We had a special reason for not mentioning it to anyone." And she told about the missing watch.

Mr. Maypenny chuckled and shook his head. "Always some excitement around you, Trixie. Did you find the watch?"

"No, but we know who did. Dan's footprints were all around where we're sure it fell." Honey helped herself from the plate of sugar-and-cinnamon-covered doughnuts and started to nibble, while Trixie poured the milk out of the old stoneware pitcher. "Did he mention it?"

"I haven't seen the boy all morning. He was up before daylight. Skyhooted out someplace without stopping to wake me. Must be the day when people get up early!" He grinned. "You girls and Dan."

"Wonder when he'll be back." Honey frowned a little. "Should we wait, Trix, or just have Mr. Maypenny tell Dan to bring the watch to school with him tomorrow?"

As she spoke, Dan Mangan came in through the kitchen door and tossed his cap expertly toward the peg on the wall.

"Oh, here you are!" Old Mr. Maypenny dumped

another batch of hot doughnuts onto the plate. "The girls have come for Honey's watch."

"For *what?*" Dan's neck stiffened and his eyes were hard as he stared at Honey.

Honey flushed and looked uncomfortable. "Why, my watch. The one you picked up this morning at the trail crossing."

"I haven't seen your watch. And I haven't been anywhere near the trail crossing." Dan spoke angrily and glared at both the girls.

"But we saw your boot tracks all around," Trixie retorted, stung by his antagonism. "You must have been there."

Dan's eyes blazed. "First I'm a liar because you think you saw me someplace yesterday where I wasn't. Now you're calling me a thief! You two are just looking for trouble, and if you keep on, you're going to get it!"

"Daniel!" Mr. Maypenny shouted at him. "That's enough of that kind of talk. Are you forgetting—?" He broke off suddenly, and in a moment went on in a milder tone. "Calm down, boy. It's a misunderstanding. Honey and Trixie, tell Dan about the watch."

"I don't know as I want to hear," Dan snarled angrily. "It's nothing to me."

"I'm sorry, Dan. Nobody meant to accuse you of

stealing a thing," Honey said gently. Then as Dan, calmed by her friendly tone, listened reluctantly, Honey explained about the loss of the watch. "So we were hoping madly you'd found it!" she concluded.

"Well, I didn't," Dan muttered. Then he cast a look at Trixie, who was still regarding him doubtfully. "Even though certain parties would like to say so!"

He grabbed for his cap and stalked out, slamming the door behind him. The two girls looked at each other. Trixie shrugged. So far as she was concerned, those bootmarks meant he had been there at the cross-trails. But Honey looked worried and unhappy.

A few minutes later, as they cantered along the main trail that led out into Glen Road across from Mr. Lytell's general store, Honey answered shortly and absentmindedly as Trixie rattled off a list of the things she intended to buy there. "And some old-fashioned peppermint sticks for Bobby. Moms asked me last week to *puh-leeze* remember to get them next time we rode that way. She's going to break up a couple of them into the ice-cream freezer next time she makes ice cream for dessert. Dad loves peppermint ice cream."

"Mmm-hmm," Honey answered politely, but her mind was afar off. "Trixie, I get the strangest feeling about Dan Mangan. He's only as old as Mart, but he looks as if he had lived and lived and been *so* unhappy."

"I think he's just a tough kid who's working because he needs to make some money and he thinks it'll be easy on a farm in winter," Trixie said firmly. "Or else he's in some awful kind of trouble and he's hiding from the police!"

"Trixie!" Honey was really shocked. "That's not fair. You don't know a thing about Dan Mangan, really."

But only a few minutes later, it seemed as if Trixie might very well have guessed what he really was like. The two girls were standing in front of the counter in Mr. Lytell's store. He had just finished counting out a dozen peppermint sticks. "Anything else, ladies?" he asked, adding the candy to the small pile of purchases on the counter.

"I don't think so," Trixie said uncertainly. "Remember anything, Hon?" She turned to Honey. But Honey's shocked eyes were fixed on an object on the shelf behind the counter. It was a wrist watch. Honey's watch!

"Mr. Lytell! Where did you get the watch?" Trixie demanded sharply.

Mr. Lytell picked it up and swung it by the gold band. "This? Some young feller in a black leather jacket sold it to me this morning for ten dollars."

"Not Dan Mangan?" Trixie asked, horrified.

"I don't know anybody by that name. This was a dark-looking boy, sort of sharp-faced and skinny. Said he was eloping and this watch belonged to his girl and they'd run out of money."

Chapter 12
Strong Evidence

"But that is a big story!" Honey protested. "That's my very own watch that I lost yesterday in the woods! Isn't it, Trixie?"

"Of course!" Trixie backed her up. "If you'll look inside, you'll see some writing. What does it say, Honey?"

"It says 'For Madeleine with Love, Mum and Daddy.' Mother's name is Madeleine, like my really true one. *Her* folks gave her the watch when she graduated from finishing school."

Mr. Lytell opened the back of the watch carefully, shoved his glasses up onto his forehead, and studied the writing inside the case. Then he adjusted the glasses, snapped the case shut, and offered the watch to Honey. "It's yours, all right, Honey, sure as shootin'."

Honey drew back. "It's yours now, Mr. Lytell. You bought it in good faith."

Lytell shook his gray head emphatically. "Nope. I gave a young feller ten dollars for it, but it isn't right-fully mine. To tell the truth, I didn't think it was worth even that much. Thought it was silver-plated. But the boy looked sort of peaked and desperate, and I figured he needed money bad. Guess he was laughing at me all the time, the scalawag." He sighed. "Take it, and don't be so careless next time."

"But your ten dollars—" Honey stammered. "I haven't that much right now. You'll have to wait till Dad and Mother come home from their trip before I can pay you back."

"I guess my whiskers won't grow too long, waitin'," the storekeeper chuckled. "Something tells me Miss Trask will be coming by here right soon, with a ten-dollar bill in her pretty hand. And don't forget to tell her I'm planning to brew a good strong pot of tea and serve genuine imported English tea biscuits when she comes. Don't forget that, now."

"I won't, Mr. Lytell." Honey was fastening the clasp of the watch band as she spoke. "And thanks a lot."

"By the way, Trixie, what did you say was the name of that young feller you thought might be Mr. Black Jacket? Guess I'd better phone Police Chief Moran to look him up if he's still around. A good talking to wouldn't be out of line."

"But he didn't actually *steal* my watch," Honey said earnestly. "He only *found* it."

"He knew he should have inquired around to find out who'd lost it," Trixie said sharply. "I guess that's why he didn't tell the truth about finding it. He wanted money for it. So he practically stole it."

"Looks like that to me, too," Mr. Lytell growled. "What did you say his name is?"

"Dan M—" Trixie began.

Honey interrupted her hastily. "Even if this person could be called a thief, we have no real evidence that he's Dan, Trixie."

"But, Honey," Trixie frowned, "nobody else around here wears pointed-toe Western riding boots except Dan Mangan!"

They hadn't noticed the door opening, or Bill Regan standing in the doorway listening with a scowl. He came toward them with a quick stride. "What was that about Dan Mangan? What has the boy been up to?"

Before either of the surprised girls could explain, the storekeeper chuckled. "The young ladies don't seem to agree on whether he's done anything or not."

"Suppose you tell me about it," Regan said curtly to them. "Start at the beginning."

So they did, and Regan's face grew whiter and more severe-looking as Trixie insisted that she was sure the seller of the watch had been Dan.

"But I don't think we can be sure," Honey objected. "Why don't we just forget the whole thing?"

Bill Regan shook his head slowly. "I'll have a talk with him tonight and with Maypenny. I'll get the truth, and if it's as Trixie here believes, Maypenny will have to send him back where he came from." But he sighed as he spoke, both girls noticed.

"Maybe he *did* sell it," Honey said stubbornly, "but maybe he needed the money badly for something."

"The boy has an honest job here, Honey. If he needed money for something important, Maypenny would have advanced it to him, I know." He looked grim. "I'm afraid Dan's an experiment that failed." He turned on his heel and stalked across the floor and out the front door.

Trixie was wearing an excited look as Honey turned to her. "Now what?" Honey asked a little impatiently.

"He called Dan *an experiment!* Remember what Bobby said about a 'dangerous sperimen' that Regan and Tom Delanoy were bringing back from the city? They must have meant Dan!"

"But what would that mean? And why should they call it dangerous?" Honey frowned. "He's just a kid."

"And why would Regan have told Moms that he

didn't want us to know anything about it?" Trixie puzzled. "And he was awfully worried."

Mr. Lytell chuckled. "Seems to me the best way to find out what other people's private conversations are about is to ask them. And if they don't want to tell, seems to me it's polite not to go poking around trying to find out."

"You're right, of course, Mr. Lytell," Honey admitted. "But we don't mean any harm. We're just wondering."

"And we're a little mixed up right now," Trixie added with a sigh. "So standing around maybe-ing won't help."

They said a hasty good-by to Mr. Lytell, gathered up the peppermint sticks and other small items, and left for home.

"Yeeks! When I think of all the housework waiting for me, I practically die!" Trixie moaned as they cantered along Glen Road.

"We'll divide it up and get through in nothing flat," Honey laughed.

"If I had a houseful of servants like you have, I'd never ruin my lily-white hands doing a single dish! And sewing! I just can't get over the way you can sew and patch and do all those things. Why, even Aunt Alicia, when she looked at the lining of my B.W.G. coat, thought it had been tailor-made at some fancy shop!"

"I thank you for the kind letter of recommendation," Honey laughed. They rode on together till they came to the Wheeler driveway and a clear view of the clubhouse.

Jim and Brian were just coming out. "Hey! Where have you two been? We've been waiting for you to come and start painting!" Jim called, shaking his finger at them.

Honey spoke quickly to Trixie. "Do we have to tell them about my watch right now? They might get angry with Dan if we tell them we suspect him."

Trixie hesitated. "All we could tell them, honestly, is that you lost it and *somebody* found it and you got it back. And they'd tease you about being careless."

"Thanks, Trix. That's how I felt. It doesn't seem fair to drag Dan Mangan's name into it till we *know.*"

"Why the deep conference?" Brian laughed as he and Jim came up to them. "Why so serious?"

"If you had to make five or six beds before lunch, you'd look serious, too. To say nothing about getting lunch ready for some half-starved characters like I see before me!" Trixie answered saucily.

"Sounds like a hint she needs help. Shall we sacrifice ourselves on the household altar?" Jim asked with a twinkle.

"The offer's accepted, with thanks!" Trixie giggled. "They've promised to unsaddle for us and clean the tack." She swung out of her saddle. "Let's give them a chance to be our heroes!"

"Pure gall!" sighed Jim. "But I'm afraid it's our only chance of getting fed today. Run along, little ones!" He helped his adopted sister lightly out of her saddle. "And now, scoot, both of you! We'll expect a feast for the gods in half an hour!"

"You'll get ham sandwiches and milk in about an *hour,* or fix your own lunches!" Trixie retorted.

"And make plenty while you're at it!" Jim called after them, while Brian stood by smiling.

It was a couple of hours later that the girls got back to the little clubhouse to start their painting. They found that Jim had done an excellent job of sketching the Mexican figures and blocking in the words announcing the date of the ice festival. The girls went to work at once, splashing gay colors on the cardboard.

Early winter darkness was beginning to settle around the small cottage as they finished several posters and laid them aside to dry.

The boys had gone to the lake with the first load of

rough planks that were to become booths for the carnival. Brian was driving his jalopy with Jim beside him, and Mart, well-bundled, perched on top of the lumber.

"There, that's the end!" Trixie added a final dab of bright crimson poster paint to the skirt of a dancing *señorita*. "How's this? It sort of hits you in the eye with all the reds and greens, doesn't it?"

"I think it's gorgeous," Honey said loyally. "Besides, red and green are Mexican colors, and it was clever of you to use so much of them—"

All at once the wind struck the small window that faced toward the driveway and rattled it as if a fist had banged on it. Both girls jumped and stared, frightened, at the window. Then the wind rattled it again and they saw there was no one glaring in at them. Only darkness.

"Sounds like the start of another storm," Trixie exclaimed. She hurried to the window and peered out. "It's beginning to snow. Guess we'd better start for home now." She pressed closer to the pane and shielded her eyes from the lamplight. "Somebody's riding up. It's Regan!"

"I suppose he jumped all over poor Dan," Honey said unhappily. "I wish I hadn't told Mr. Lytell it was my watch."

"But you had to, Honey," Trixie reminded her

soberly. "It's too bad about Dan Mangan, especially if he's Mr. Maypenny's grandson, but I guess Regan and your dad have a right to want people they can trust around the place."

She went to the door to open it for Regan. The snow was driving hard as the tall red-haired groom came up. His head and shoulders were whitened by it as if someone had sprinkled powdered sugar over them. Trixie couldn't help noticing it and she was about to mention it, when she saw his grim expression. She said hastily, "Come in. We saw you ride up."

"No time to visit. I've been longer than I expected," Regan said brusquely. "I thought maybe I'd find some of you kids here. I wanted to tell you that you won't have any more trouble with Dan Mangan. Mr. Maypenny will be sending him away before the end of the week. That's all."

He turned abruptly and started back to his horse.

Trixie ran after him impulsively, ignoring the snow that fell on her bare head. She called, "Please wait a minute." And when Regan, stony-faced, waited to hear what was on her mind, she asked quickly, "Did Dan tell you he *was* the one who found Honey's watch and sold it?"

Even in the semidarkness, his face looked stern.

"No, Trixie. He hadn't the grace to admit it. But I looked at those bootmarks on the ground where she lost the watch, and he might as well have signed his name."

"Honey still thinks it might have been somebody else," Trixie suggested. "Other boys wear boots like that."

But Regan shook his head. "In the city, maybe. Not out here." He turned toward Jupiter, and Trixie heard him say, half under his breath, "I guess we were foolish to expect anything else."

Trixie went back into the little clubhouse shaking off the snowflakes. She was shivering with cold.

"I guess there's no doubt about Dan," Honey sighed. "But somehow, I feel terribly disappointed. Poor Mr. Maypenny! How he must hate to send Dan away!"

"How Dan must hate to be sent away! He's been having a ball, swaggering around the other kids at school, telling what a big shot he was in the city. I bet he'll be simply furious at us! There's no telling what he might do for revenge!" Trixie's imagination was making her shiver even more than the wet snowflakes were.

Honey laughed. "Now you're taking his wild stories seriously! I still think he isn't half as dangerous as he pretends to be! He just made up those yarns."

But when they and the boys stopped by the clubhouse the next morning to pick up the finished posters and take them to Sleepyside on the bus, they changed their minds about Dan's boasting and bragging about being tough. Perhaps he *had* been telling the truth after all!

Chapter 13
A Thief in the Night

It had stopped snowing some time in the night and there were only a few inches of snow carpeting the ground around the small clubhouse when they came up outside.

"I'll dash in and get the posters," Mart offered and cut across the smooth expanse of snow toward the front door.

The others waited for him to reappear, Brian glancing with a frown at his watch while they stood around. "Mart! What's keeping you?" he called.

Trixie giggled. "Another black bear?" she grinned at Jim.

"No bear of mine this time," Jim laughed. But he stopped laughing abruptly as Mart appeared in the doorway and called out in an oddly strained voice, "Hey, come in here!"

"We're late now. We'll miss the bus!" Brian yelled back. "Come on, and cut the clowning."

"Better take a look," Mart answered seriously. "We've had a visitor."

They exchanged worried glances as they hurried to

see what he meant. And when they looked around inside the usually neat little cottage, they were dismayed at the wreckage someone had left.

"Looks like one of us left the front door unlocked last night," Jim said with a frown.

"Not us!" Trixie defended herself and Honey at once. "We put the catch on the lock, and I closed the door tight after us. Then Honey tried the knob and it was locked. We always do it that way, so neither of us is responsible alone for seeing that it's locked."

"Somebody goofed this time," Mart said grimly. "Wow! Posters spread around on the floor, paint pots tipped over, curtains torn. Looks as if our visitor had a grudge against one or all of us!"

A light gust of wind blew in the curtain at the window through which Trixie had watched Regan ride up last night. Trixie glanced at it, feeling the draft. "Hey, the window's broken. That's how they got in, whoever they were!"

Brian hurried over and found one pane broken. "You're right, Trixie. This pane has been smashed so they could reach in and unlock the window. And the snow's been wiped off the sill, probably by somebody's hand. I wish one of us knew something about taking fingerprints."

Trixie said, "Oh!" suddenly and darted behind the partition. They heard her rummaging around back there as if she were looking for something. Then she exclaimed, "I knew it!" and a moment later came rushing out with the small tin box that they called the Temper Box. Whenever one of them lost his or her temper, that one had to put a dime in the box as a penalty. There had been three dollars and forty cents in the box. It was empty now.

"Of all the nasty, cheap, miserable tricks! It isn't the money that makes me mad," she stormed, "but he had to break the lock and twist the cover so we can't use the box again. I'd like to break what's left of it on his head!"

"Ah, ah!" Mart said, lifting an admonishing finger at his sister. "Temper? Most of those dimes were yours, *ma petite!* Do we start a new collection right now?"

Trixie tossed her head and scowled at him, but she put the box down on the table. "I'm perfectly calm." Then she started to boil over again, "But whoever it was is a—a—"

"I agree with Trixie completely," Brian said. "Personally, I think some tramp saw this spot and decided to spend a night under a good stout roof instead of under some railroad bridge in a hobo jungle. He made himself at home."

"Like a pig in a wallow!" Jim said grimly. He picked up one of the cardboard posters and shook his head over it. "He walked all over this one with wet boots."

"Boots?" Honey said quickly before she had had time to think. She and Trixie exchanged a look and both hurried to look at the card in Jim's hands.

Clear as it could be, the imprint was of a pointed-toe and narrow-heeled boot.

"That looks familiar," Jim told them with a frown. "Whoever it was that broke in wears those corny cowboy boots like Dan Mangan's."

"*Like* them?" Trixie exploded. "I bet it *was* Dan, getting even with Honey and me!"

The three boys looked astonished. Jim spoke quickly. "Suppose you explain just why Dan Mangan would 'get even' with you. What have you been doing to him?" He was stern.

"We haven't done anything," Trixie defended herself and Honey. "He's the one that did it!"

"Suppose you start at the beginning and tell us what this is all about," Brian said seriously. "We'll probably miss the bus, but this is more important right now."

"Yeah," Mart agreed. "I want to find out if I should punch Dan Mangan in the nose when I see him in class today, or if this is just another of your pipe dreams."

So Trixie and Honey explained about the lost watch and Mr. Lytell's purchase of it. Honey added, at the end, a little defiantly, "Of course, we're not sure it was Dan who found it, but Regan seems to think so, too."

"So you dragged him into your mystery, too!" Mart shook his head.

"He just happened to hear us talking, and he blew up!" Trixie explained. All three of the boys looked so grim and disapproving that she was worried. "He's making Mr. Maypenny send Dan back to wherever he came from, next week."

"Tough break for Dan if he isn't the one who found Honey's watch," Jim said with a frown. "Personally, I don't think we should accuse him of breaking in here without a lot more evidence than you two had about the watch. It's a serious charge to base on one footprint and a suspicion of revenge."

Mart had been examining the footprint on the poster. He put the poster on the floor and measured the print against his own thick boot. "Especially when the footprint's a good inch longer than mine in my heaviest boots, and I know Dan wears a smaller size than I do!"

"Let me see!" Jim strode over and checked Mart's discovery. "You're right. Well, that changes things a bit,

I'd say. Did Lytell mention anything about the guy with the watch having extra big feet?"

Both the girls shook their heads. "Of course not," Trixie told him, "or we'd have known it wasn't Dan."

"Also, these boots were brown, not black like Dan's," Honey said, pointing to some smudges on the edge of the table. "The character, whoever he was, put his feet up and rubbed shoe polish on our clean table!"

All three of the boys checked hastily. It *was* shoe polish that was streaked on the table and some of it was rubbed on the face of one of the posters that showed a dent where a heavy heel had rested. And the polish *was* brown, a very yellowish, ugly brown.

"Anybody who'd wear this wild-looking color must be a mental case!" Mart said with a shudder. "Yikes!"

"Funny thing, I can't imagine a tramp wearing yellowish brown cowboy boots. Can you?" Brian asked Jim.

"He may not have been a tramp," Jim said gravely. "Maybe he was just passing through, hiking, and needed money, so he broke in and got three dollars and forty cents luckier."

"He didn't have to make a mess of our clubhouse, whatever his troubles were!" Trixie said, getting angry again. "Look at that heap of half-smoked cigarettes beside the stove! Ugh, the smelly things!"

"Cigarettes? There's another bit of evidence that Dan isn't the guilty party!" Jim told them quickly. "He mentioned not smoking the other day when one of the kids offered him a cigarette."

There was a distant sound of an auto horn. The bus was coming, the last bus they could catch and still get to Sleepyside High on time.

"Skedaddle, all of you! I'll straighten up around here and catch the next bus. I don't have a class till second period." Jim shooed them all out and they ran down to the bus stop just in time to board the bus and collapse breathless in their seats.

Honey and Trixie made their way to the rear so they could talk undisturbed, while Mart and Brian glanced through their math books.

"I'm glad it wasn't Dan," Honey said. "I suppose you're sort of disappointed, because you don't like him."

Trixie thought it over a moment. Then she said, "I'm not disappointed. I'm glad, same as you are. Only, not so much for Dan's sake. It's Mr. Maypenny I'm glad for."

"What has Mr. Maypenny got to do with this?" Honey was often perplexed by the way Trixie's ideas jumped all over the place.

"Don't you see?" Trixie was very earnest. "If Dan

isn't the only person around with those pointed-toe boots, then it's possible *he* didn't find your watch. And as for the boy who found it being dark and skinny like Dan, I guess there are plenty who look like that. So he's being sent away by Regan for something he didn't do, and when we go tell Mr. Maypenny that we were mistaken about Dan, why, he won't have to send Dan away after all. And if Dan's his grandson, Mr. Maypenny will be glad. See?"

Honey nodded, a little dizzily. "We're going to see him? When?"

"I thought after school, on our way to the lake for rehearsal," Trixie informed her. "And by that time we'll have told Regan, too."

But when they went to the Wheeler stables after school to get Strawberry and Lady, Regan was nowhere about. They saddled the horses, who were champing at the bit to get started on their airing. The boys were already out building the booths along the lakeside.

As the two girls rode out of the barn, Tom Delanoy, the chauffeur, came hurrying down from the Manor House with a message for Honey.

"Miss Trask says your folks will be home any day now, Miss Honey," Tom said respectfully. He was always a little formal with Honey, though he could unbend and laugh with the boys when they came to watch him work on the family cars. He was as friendly as Regan, but was the big redhead's exact opposite so far as coloring went. Tom had dark curly hair and blue eyes. "She's expecting a wire and will call you at Crabapple Farm when she hears which plane you're to meet."

"Oh, thanks, Tom. I'm hoping they'll get here next week for the ice carnival!"

"Where is Regan?" Trixie asked. "We want to tell him something important."

"I'm afraid you'll have to wait a bit for that, Miss Trixie," the young chauffeur told her, a frown suddenly appearing. "I put Regan on the train to town this morning. Something came up sudden that he has to tend to."

"Oh." Trixie and Honey exchanged disappointed looks.

"Your brothers were looking for him, too," Tom volunteered. "I don't know what for, but they seemed a mite upset when they found out he was gone."

"Thanks, Tom. We'll catch up with Regan when he gets back." Trixie rode down the driveway, followed by Honey.

"I wonder if Regan's gone to see somebody about sending Dan back," Trixie called to her friend. "That certainly would get things all mixed up if he makes arrangements and then we tell him we were mistaken. I mean, that *I* was mistaken. You've always stuck up for Dan."

Honey laughed. "I wasn't half as sure as I pretended. But I'm glad it's going to turn out all right for him."

"We'll tell the boys to get hold of Regan and talk to him the minute he comes back," Trixie planned. "I'm going to ask Jim if there's something Dan can do to help us get ready for the carnival. Maybe he would feel more at home if he felt we were taking him into the plans."

But when they came onto Dan in the middle of the game preserve a little later, he wasn't in the mood to be either friendly or helpful.

He had been making a snare for one of the Wheeler pheasants that was to furnish a meal for a small party of Mr. Wheeler's friends a few days later. He stood with the snare in his hands, feet planted apart as he glared defiantly at the two girls. "What do you want to talk about? I told you I've got work to do!" he barked at Trixie, who had volunteered to approach him.

"You don't need to snap my head off!" Trixie retorted. "We just wanted to tell you that we've decided that it was somebody else who found Honey's watch and sold it to Mr. Lytell. Not you."

164

"What am I supposed to say? 'Thank you, ma'am'?"

"Of course not!" Honey rode a few feet closer to the dark-faced boy and smiled down at him. "We just want you to know that we're going to tell Mr. Maypenny right now that we're sure we were mistaken."

"Don't bother!" he snapped, with a scowl. "I'm getting out of this backwoods joint in a couple of days, and what that old square thinks about me means exactly zero." He turned his back on her and went to work on the snare.

Honey hesitated a moment, and though Trixie couldn't see her face, she felt sure Honey had tears in her eyes. She wasn't used to being talked to like that.

"Come on, Honey," Trix called to her friend. "Let's leave before Mr. Hydrophobia gets sore enough to bite one of us!"

Honey wheeled Lady and rode away without speaking, but Trixie saw her dash a tear from her eye with the back of her hand.

"I have a good mind not to tell Mr. Maypenny we may have been wrong about that—that character!" Trixie sputtered as they rode side by side.

"Oh, no! We *must* tell him. And Regan, too. It doesn't matter if Dan wants to be disagreeable. I guess we can't blame him too much, if he's innocent."

165

"I suppose not," Trixie admitted grudgingly. Then she started up the narrowing trail.

But Honey pulled in and looked back at Dan Mangan. Sunlight was slanting down through the tall evergreens, and a shaft of it struck Dan as he stood looking after them with drooping shoulders. On an impulse, she waved.

To her surprise, Dan snatched off his cap and waved in answer. "He's up at Storm King hunting for that wildcat!" he called, cupping his hands around his mouth.

"We'll find him. Thanks!" Honey called back, and waved again before she wheeled her horse and followed Trixie.

Chapter 14
Mr. Maypenny's Accident

"You see! Dan *does* want us to tell Mr. Maypenny what we found out. That means he wouldn't have been so glad to be sent back to wherever-it-is! I'm glad I waved to him!" Honey's eyes sparkled.

Trixie only said *"Hrmph!"* and kept riding along. They were getting close to the clearing that surrounded the sturdy little log cabin that Mr. Maypenny's grandfather had built almost a hundred years ago. There was no smoke coming out of the cobblestone chimney, so they knew that he hadn't yet returned from the hunting expedition.

Trixie glanced at her wrist watch. "I don't think we'll wait too long. We want to be at the lake well before sunset. I hope the boys have a nice big fire going."

They dismounted to give the horses a rest while they waited. In a few minutes, Mr. Maypenny, astride old Brownie, rode in from the north trail that led through the woods into the labyrinth and beyond that toward the high peaks.

"Glad to see you youngsters," he said. "Didn't the boy ask you inside?"

"He's away back there, fixing a snare," Trixie explained. "We don't have much time anyhow. We just wanted to talk to you a few minutes."

"Good! If you'll just wait till I put away my gear and settle this old nag of mine in the barn, I'll be with you. Go on in and light the fire for some hot soup or a cup of chocolate."

"Never mind the food," Trixie told him cheerfully. "We'll come along with you and talk there."

"All right, if that's how you want it," he agreed, chuckling. "First time I've heard Miss Trix turn down hot chocolate! Must be something important on your mind."

"We think so," Trixie grinned. "I guess you will, too."

They walked toward the barn with him, and they told him their reasons for thinking they had made a mistake by identifying Dan as the person who had sold Honey's watch to Mr. Lytell.

"It was on account of those weird cowboy boots he wears that we blamed Dan," Trixie said honestly. "Now we've found out there's somebody else who wears the same kind, but a much larger size. And whoever it was broke into our clubhouse last night and stole some money and just about wrecked the place."

When they had finished telling him about it, the old man was silent a moment. When he spoke again, there was a brighter gleam in his eyes. "Thanks, little ladies, for coming all this way to tell me. The boy will be glad to hear what you've found out. And so will Regan when the poor lad gets back from the city. It's too bad he couldn't have heard the news before he left!"

Trixie was eager to ask him some questions, but they had reached the barn, and he turned briskly to them as he paused at the doorway. "Sure you won't stay for a hot drink? It's mighty chilly."

"No, thanks," Trixie told him. "We're on our way to the lake for a bonfire party with the boys, and to practice some new figures for the carnival next week."

"Well, run right along. Me, I'm going to go bring that young Dan home, and we'll have some good hunters' stew while I tell him what you've told me."

"I hope he listens a little better to you than he did to us!" Trixie said, still smarting from Dan's treatment.

"I'm sure he will," Honey said, with a smile.

"He's a strange one, all right," Mr. Maypenny chuckled. "Kinda short-tempered, but not as bad as he thinks!"

He held their horses as they mounted, and nodded toward the half moon in the darkening sky. "Looks like a bright, clear evening. Have yourselves some fun!"

Trixie glanced toward the woods in the direction of the high mountains. "Did you see anything of our catamount?"

"Almost caught up with him," he said. "Tracked him five miles beyond Storm King and only saw him once. Took a shot, but he was moving too fast for me, covering twenty feet at a jump. I didn't have the heart to chase him any farther, seeing that the big feller was headed away from here up toward the high peaks. Guess that's where he's got his family."

The girls looked toward the distant mountains, hardly visible in the late shadows. "I hope he stays home with them now!" Trixie said with a shiver.

They rode off a moment later, and though they kept looking for another sight of Dan Mangan, they didn't get a glimpse of him.

"I still wonder what he meant by feeling sorry for *Regan*? Do you suppose that means Mr. Maypenny isn't Dan's grandfather, after all, in spite of having the same kind of chin?" Trixie asked as they turned into the cross-path that led to the lake.

"I'm sure I don't know. It *is* sort of odd that Regan had to go to the city about Dan," Honey said, with a frown. "At least, Mr. Maypenny practically *said* he did."

They found a brisk bonfire on the lake shore, and the booths all standing, finished except for the bunting and the games and souvenirs they expected to have.

"You are simply wonderful!" Honey told the three boys.

Trixie was walking around the largest booth, inspecting it. "I see you signed your work, too." Her voice came from behind the big wooden structure. "Which one of you calls himself Ymca?" Her grin appeared over the top of the booth.

"She's got us!" Jim laughed. "You win, Trix. We did get a little lift here and there. We borrowed that one, I admit. It was left over from a party at the Y.M.C.A.! Di's father hauled it over, as is, a while ago."

"Well, now I feel much better," Trixie said. "We were just going to offer to do some extra work so you could rest after your labors. Now we'll merely inquire where all the hot dogs and hamburgers are stacked, and how soon you'll be serving your hungry guests."

"Unfair!" Mart bellowed. "You'll cook your own, princess! All you've done is ride around visiting. I bet you stopped at old Maypenny's for some of that hot chocolate that's going to make you both look like bags of potatoes if you keep it up!"

"At least we're not growing out of our B.W.G. jackets as fast as *some* persons!" Trixie retorted. "And that gives me a precious idea for the carnival! Why don't you wear last year's Sunday suit and be a clown? Those bony wrists and the jacket that doesn't come near touching the top of your trousers should be a scream!"

"Since Brian and I are running this carnival—" Jim began sternly.

"Who said so?" Trixie asked pertly. "It was *our* idea."

"I repeat," Jim scowled playfully at her, "since we strong masculine types have to do all the work, and be insulted into the bargain, the least you squaws could do would be to rustle up the eats."

"Come on, Trix, I think my big brother has a point there," Honey laughed.

"All right, but we won't tell them what Mr. Maypenny said, just for that," Trixie said with a sniff.

"Okay, get the frying pan to work, and we'll try to keep from dying of curiosity," Brian said drily. "As a matter of fact, I don't believe you even saw Mr. Maypenny. You'd still be there gobbling his stew."

"But we did see him, really. And we told him we had decided it was somebody besides Dan who sold my watch," Honey told him earnestly.

"Did Dan forgive you?" Mart grinned. "Bet he just hissed at you and coiled up."

"That's a mean remark," Honey said, with as much anger as any of them had ever seen her show. "It's not fair."

"I'm sorry," Mart said humbly. "I was just being a clown. I guess it comes natural to me. I don't really feel that way about Dan Mangan."

"I hope not," Jim said seriously. "I think we ought to do something to show we're sorry we misjudged him."

"We could ask him to come and have some of our supper here tonight," Trixie suggested. "Though I know he'd say No."

"He might not," Honey argued. "He waved to me and told us where to find Mr. Maypenny, remember."

The boys exchanged looks. "All right. Tell us the story of your gay afternoon in the woods. Let the hamburgers and hot dogs wait." Mart pulled at a stray blond curl that had escaped from Trixie's head scarf.

But when the girls had told about the talk with Mr. Maypenny, including his strange sympathy for "poor lad" Regan, the boys had no more idea than they what he had meant.

"Anyhow," Brian told them when they had given up

guessing, "one of us should go on over to Maypenny's and talk to Dan. And it wouldn't do any harm, if he's at all friendly, to invite him to bring his skates and take a few turns around the lake. It might break the ice."

"That's what we need, broken ice to skate on," Mart grinned at his big brother.

"Smarty! We know what Brian meant, if *you* don't," Trixie sniffed at him. "And just for that, *you* ought to be the one who goes to Maypenny's and talks to Dan. Does everybody agree? All in favor, say Aye!"

And before he could beg off, a chorus of Ayes from the other four members of the Bob-Whites elected him their messenger, although he sputtered protests.

Still grumbling, he left the warm circle of the fire and mounted Jupiter. "If I come back fast, he took a pitchfork to me!" he called to them as he rode into the darkness of the trail.

It was less than fifteen minutes later that they heard him come riding down the trail a lot faster than he had gone up it. When he was still a score of yards away, he called out, "Jim! Brian! Come here!"

There was such an edge of excitement in his voice that the two boys looked at each other in sudden alarm. "Sounds like trouble!" Jim exclaimed, setting aside the frying pan he was holding over the fire. "Let's go!"

But the girls were right on their heels when they reached Mart as he swung off Jupiter, panting for breath.

"Mr. Maypenny! There's been an accident!"

"Where?" Jim asked at once.

"Mr. Maypenny?" the two girls chorused.

Mart nodded.

"Where is he?" Brian was the only calm one. "Let's go, boys. Girls, you'd better stay here and tend the fire. We'll be back as soon as possible."

"What happened to him, Mart?" Trixie insisted, holding on to Mart's sleeve as the others started to mount.

"Looks as if a branch broke off one of the blue spruces, about half a mile from his house. I don't know what he was doing out there this time of night, but it seems to have hit him on the head. He's got a nasty gash and he's unconscious," Mart told them.

Trixie and Honey looked at each other as Mart hurriedly mounted to join his brother and Jim Frayne.

"He said he was going out to get Dan," Trixie reminded Honey. "I hope they didn't have an argument."

"Oh, Trixie! Don't even think such a thing!" Honey moaned.

"Well, I'm not going to stay here and just wait and

176

worry. I'm going to find out if there's something we can do." Trixie started away, but Honey held her arm.

"I'll dump snow on the fire. You wrap up all the food and we'll put it in the boathouse so the porcupines won't get at it." Honey was always practical.

"Okay, but let's hurry!"

When they caught up with the boys at the junction of one of the trails and a narrow path, the three were grouped around the unconscious figure of Mr. Maypenny in the light of two flashlights.

The girls dismounted and tied their horses beside the boys' three. They were almost afraid to go look, but after a moment's hesitation, Trixie took Honey's hand and they hurried over together.

Brian, his face grave, was kneeling beside Mr. Maypenny, carefully examining the gamekeeper's scalp. Jim and Mart crouched close by.

"He'll need some stitches," Brian said softly, "but there doesn't seem to be a concussion. Let's get him to the house where we can make him comfortable till a doctor can get there."

The old man groaned and opened his eyes. "Never mind—a doctor—" he whispered. "I'm a tough old nut and my head's the same!" And he even grinned bravely as he struggled to rise to a sitting position.

"Better just lie quiet and we'll make you a litter, sir," Brian advised.

"Nonsense!" Mr. Maypenny was getting stronger by the minute. He sat up, gingerly feeling the wound, but reassured by touch that it wasn't too serious. "I've had a worse head from falling off old Brownie." He squinted up at the evergreen, with its snow-laden branches, that towered over them. "Dratted tree!"

Against their better judgment, the boys helped him to his feet, and started up the trail toward his cabin, one on each side. Mart and the girls followed silently.

"Stubborn old coot!" Mart whispered as they came in sight of the cabin. "How does he know he doesn't have a broken skull?"

But Trixie shushed him abruptly. "*Some* people *know* when they're 'cracked,'" she told him with an impish grin, "and others don't!"

Honey was staring at the house, where the lights seemed to be on not only in the kitchen but in the bedroom and the living-room and even in the low-roofed attic where a single electric light shone out onto the snow through a tiny square window above the rear door. "Goodness!" she exclaimed. "I wonder why Dan's got every light in the house turned on!"

"Maybe he came home and found Mr. Maypenny

gone, and he's looking around there for him!" Trixie suggested.

The tall boys helped the owner of the house up to the front door, and Jim tried the doorknob. The lock was on.

"Hey, Dan! Open up! Mr. Maypenny's been hurt!" Brian called.

They heard the high-heeled boots cross the floor, and a moment later the door was flung open to silhouette Dan Mangan.

"A tree branch fell on him. It's just a cut, I think," Brian explained hastily, "but I'd better take a couple of stitches." He helped Mr. Maypenny up the single step.

Dan stood barring the door. He took Mr. Maypenny's arm and drew him in. "I'll take care of him. I know how. Thanks for your help," he said brusquely, "but you can go now!"

Chapter 15
A New Mystery

For a moment both Jim and Brian were too astounded to speak. Dan's unfriendly manner and his sharp words were a shock. They stood staring at him as he held Mr. Maypenny's arm and started to reach for the door with his other hand, to close it on them.

"Just a minute, bud," Brian said grimly. He stuck his heavy boot over the threshold so the door wouldn't close and pushed forward. "I'm not so sure you know how to take care of Mr. Maypenny, and we're not going to take any chances on it."

"Get out, all of you!" Dan's face was white and drawn and his dark eyes flashed in anger. "We don't need your help!" But as he spoke, the old man sagged against him, and Dan was nearly borne down by his weight.

Without any further argument, Brian nodded to Jim, and together they lifted Mr. Maypenny and carried him across the room to the bunk against the wall. They let him down gently, and Brian started to remove the old man's coat with Jim's help.

Dan came and stood over them angrily. "Let him alone and get out of here, I said! We don't need you."

"Just keep out of the way!" Brian told him sharply and brushed him aside. "Trixie, get into the kitchen and start some water boiling. We'll have to find some bandages, too. I'm sure he has some around somewhere."

"Okay, Doc!" Trixie threw him a fleeting grin and hurried out to the kitchen. In a minute, the sound of the electric pump told them she was obeying orders.

"There's a first-aid kit in the bathroom," Dan said sullenly. "I'll bring it." And he stalked across the room.

The old gamekeeper was groaning now. The trip had been almost too much for him, in spite of his boasting. The blow had made him lose considerable blood, and he had lain out in the cold too long for safety.

"Just take it easy as you can, sir," Jim advised him, as the old man tossed in his bunk. "We'll have this fixed up in a minute or so."

Honey had been standing around looking sympathetic but helpless. She whispered hurriedly to the two boys, "What can I do to help?"

It was Brian who answered promptly. "Sterilize a needle and heavy thread in the water as soon as Trixie gets it boiling. Wash your hands well first." He turned back to the injured man without noticing that Honey looked more helpless than ever.

She wanted to ask how long it had to be in the water and how she should carry it, but she didn't want the boys to know how ignorant she was. Then and there she made up her mind to start first-aid instruction when the new class started at school. "Dope!" she called herself as she hurried to the kitchen to ask Trixie what to do.

She was in such a hurry that as she went past a small side table beside Mr. Maypenny's favorite rocker, she brushed against it and tipped it over. A quick swoop saved it from falling to the floor, but she couldn't manage to catch the small Staffordshire pottery bowl that had been sitting on it. The bowl fell to the floor and smashed, and a collection of cigarette butts scattered out of it.

"Bother!" Honey surveyed the mess and looked around for a whisk broom and dustpan. A newspaper was handy and served as both broom and pan to gather up the smelly debris. And she was all the more upset to notice that the boys were staring disapprovingly at her.

As quickly as possible she fled to the kitchen with the newspaper wadded up. "What's that?" Trixie asked, as Honey marched over to the trash basket and emptied the newspaper into it.

The water was beginning to get hot in the little kettle and Trixie was looking for a basin to carry it in.

"Cigarette stubs! Smelly!" Honey shuddered with distaste.

"Where on earth did you find those *here?*" Trixie's blue eyes opened wide in amazement. "Mr. Maypenny doesn't smoke and neither does Dan Mangan. And Mr. Maypenny has fits if anybody else smokes in his house."

"I guess he's changed his mind since Dan's been here. Or else Dan hasn't been telling the truth and *is* a smoker," Honey guessed. "They were in the little bowl that sat on the table by his chair. I broke the bowl just now and these icky things fell out—" She wrinkled her nose.

Trixie looked thoughtful a moment, then she darted to the trash basket, reached in, and brought out one of the cigarette stubs. She held it gingerly in her fingers as she read out the brand name on it. Her face was grave as she turned to Honey. "It's the same brand we found in the clubhouse. I guess this pins the blame for that right back on Dan."

Honey sighed. "I hate to admit it, but it does look bad for him. The worst is stealing our poor little three dollars and forty cents! It's so small and petty."

"Not if he needed money for cigarettes and only had enough allowance or wages to pay for his school lunch and the bus." Trixie knitted her brows over it.

"He certainly is acting awfully strange about letting the boys help Mr. Maypenny!" Honey said thoughtfully. "Do you suppose—oh, I shouldn't even think such things about the poor boy, but—do you suppose he has stolen things from us that we haven't missed yet, and he didn't want us to see them here? Like skates or some of our summer stuff?"

"Wouldn't be surprised," Trixie answered soberly. "I'm going to keep my eyes open, and if I see anything which belongs to one of us—" She broke off, suddenly aware that the door to the living-room was open and Dan was standing in the doorway scowling at her. There was no doubt he had heard her words. For a moment he just glared, while both girls looked guilty, then he said sharply, "What about the hot water? You dames going to take all day getting it?"

"Tell Brian we'll bring it right now!" Trixie managed to find her tongue.

Dan gave them a sour look, turned on his heel, and left.

They scurried about, found a needle and thread,

and sterilized them in the boiling water from the kettle. But even before they had finished, Brian himself stalked in and took over. After washing his own hands thoroughly in the best surgical style he could remember seeing on TV, he left for the living-room followed by Trixie bearing the basin of hot water and Honey carrying the needle and thread on a pad of sterile gauze.

But when Brian went to work on Mr. Maypenny's injury, the two, at Jim's suggestion, fled back to the kitchen.

They sat by the kitchen table to talk over the latest twist in their mystery.

"I suppose there's no doubt Dan's the one," Trixie said with a shake of her head. "I wonder what we should say to Regan when he gets back!"

"I think this is one time we ought to talk it over with the boys first," Honey advised seriously. "After all, this isn't all *our* business—" She stopped abruptly and stared at the ceiling. "Did you hear that? It sounded like a footstep up there?"

"No," Trixie admitted, staring at the ceiling. But she had no sooner answered than there was a sound that could have come from a creaking board in the attic. Trixie turned a startled face to Honey. "It *did* sound like a footstep!"

"There was a light up there when we rode up," Honey said with growing excitement. "Remember?"

They stopped speaking to listen again, but there was no other sound from above. The boys were talking cheerfully in the living-room, but neither Trixie nor Honey heard Dan's voice. "Maybe it's Dan up there!" Trixie said suddenly. "I don't hear him. Maybe he climbed the ladder to get away from us 'snoops' and is sulking in his castle up there!" She giggled.

But a couple of minutes later when they went back into the living-room, Dan was seated frowning at Jim and Brian as they took care of Mr. Maypenny's gashed scalp. He had slid down in his chair with his feet stuck out in their pointed-toe black boots so that the girls had to walk around him to approach Mr. Maypenny's bunk.

Trixie cast a quick look at the ladder, in a far corner of the room, that led up to the attic. The trap door at the head of the ladder was closed and even at a brief glance she could see that the hook was firmly caught in the eyebolt. When the trap door was fastened this way from below, no one could move it from above. So it was clear, she decided firmly, that there couldn't be anyone up there. As for the light that Honey thought she had seen shining out of the attic as they rode up, she probably was mistaken. They were all so excited about poor

Mr. Maypenny that Honey must have imagined it.

Mr. Maypenny had managed to be very brave. He even laughed off the idea that his head hurt. But after it was bandaged, and he could lie back and close his eyes and relax, he seemed very glad to be quiet.

"You'll be all right, sir, if you'll just rest here till morning. I wouldn't get up and wander around if I were you. You're likely to get dizzy," Brian told him.

Mr. Maypenny answered faintly, "I'll get along, boy. And much obliged for the bandagin'. The lad here will take care of me now." He opened his eyes and smiled toward Dan, then closed them and turned his head away again with a half-groan.

"Think we ought to phone Doc Tremaine to ride over and see him in the morning?" Jim whispered to Brian.

But it wasn't Brian who answered. It was Dan Mangan. "You heard what Mr. Maypenny said," Dan told them defiantly. "I can look out for him if he needs it. You just forget about calling any doctor!"

"What do you know about head injuries?" Brian asked sharply.

"I've been conked on the bean a couple of times," Dan told him with a scowl. "I didn't have to drag in a sawbones to cure me." He gestured toward the door.

"Why don't the bunch of you get out? You rich kids always got to play it your way. Nobody else knows anything. Big men!"

"Rich kids! Boy!" Mart had been silent as long as he could stand it. He faced Dan with disgust. "Boy! Are you misinformed. We Beldens aren't rich. I wish we were—I'm lazy. But we live on a farm, and all of us kids work hard to make it go."

"And our dad puts in eight hours a day on his job at the bank, sometimes lots longer," Trixie cut in, "for *his* salary!"

Dan glowered at her. "What about him?" He nodded toward Jim. "And Honey? They're rollin' in it!"

"Jim was worse off than you've ever been," Brian said quietly, "not many months ago."

Dan scowled at Jim, who smiled and nodded. "Broke, runaway, and scared. And I haven't forgotten it. But I think it would do Mr. Maypenny a lot more good if we got out of here than it will if we stand around arguing."

"Come on, kids." Brian shooed the girls and Mart toward the front door.

Trixie stopped near the door after Honey had gone out. She looked back at Dan with fire in her eyes. "You *do* hiss and coil like a snake. A copperhead!" As she finished speaking, she turned and flounced toward the door where Brian was waiting. She wasn't looking where she was going, and she bumped her shin on a chair. It hurt so much that she said, "Ouch!" and grabbed the back of the chair to support herself while she rubbed the bumped spot.

She flashed an angry look back at Dan to see if he was laughing at her and was surprised to see that he was staring with a worried expression at the chair and the object draped over the top bar that she was clutching.

The object was a black leather jacket. She forgot her aching shin. She angrily snatched the jacket off the chair and flung it at Dan. "Don't look so mean!" she stormed at him. "I was hardly touching your disgusting old jacket! I wasn't hurting it! Take a good look!"

But although Dan reached out to catch the jacket, it fell short and spread out on the floor between them. Its black, shiny back lay uppermost, and across it from shoulder to shoulder, a neatly lettered legend in white paint spelled out THE COWHANDS. And there wasn't a sign of a tear in either of the sleeves!

Chapter 16
A Terrible Discovery

Trixie stared at the black jacket spread out on the floor between her and Dan. "Why, that isn't the same ja—" she began, surprised.

Dan cut her off sharply. "Get out, will you!" he shouted, and at the same time he darted forward, snatched up the jacket, and held it behind him as he glared defiantly at her.

"Trixie!" Brian poked his head in through the doorway, "Come on! Stop squabbling, both of you! Have a little consideration for Mr. Maypenny."

She turned and went out, and a moment later Dan had slammed the door shut after them and slipped the bolt.

Brian hurried Trixie along. "We'll come back tomorrow and change the bandage, but I'm sure Mr. Maypenny will be up and around then. He's a tough old coot and it's only a scalp injury."

"It could happen to anybody after the branches get loaded with snow," Mart said. "Maybe somebody ought to advise the old boy to wear a fireman's helmet so he won't get conked again!"

All three of the boys snickered at the thought, and Honey giggled with them. But Trixie, walking a little apart as they came up to the horses, didn't join in. Her thoughts were on the black jacket spread on the cabin floor and the way Dan had acted.

As Jim settled in the saddle, he glanced back at the cabin and shook his head. "I wish there were some way to get through to Dan. Something's bothering him a lot, and if he could just talk it out to somebody, he'd be a lot better off." He paused, then added, "Dan needs friends."

"He needs a good punch in the nose!" Mart contradicted him grimly.

"He had no right to shout at Trixie that way!" Honey said from beside them as they all rode down the trail. "He's just hopeless, that's all! And I wish he would go back where he came from!"

"I thought you girls were all for Dan, now that we've decided he didn't break into the clubhouse?" Brian teased her.

"We're not so sure now," Honey said quickly. "There were cigarette butts in the bowl I broke. And they were the same kind as we found in the clubhouse."

Mart hooted. "Ye gods and little fishes! Those cigs sell a million packs a week! How do you know Mr. Lytell hadn't been calling on Maypenny lately?"

"Does he smoke that kind?" Trixie asked. She had kept out of the conversation till now.

"Who knows? I know if he does, Maypenny wouldn't have stopped him from smoking them there, even though he's so set against tobacco."

"We hadn't thought of that," Honey said with a little sigh of relief, and smiled.

"Besides, what about the brown boots our thief was wearing, two sizes larger than Dan wears?" Jim asked quietly over the clop-clop of the hoofs.

"That's right," Honey agreed cheerfully, "I forgot all about them. Didn't you, Trixie?"

"Sort of," Trixie admitted.

"Why don't you two get off Dan Mangan's back?" Mart asked with unusual gravity "Trixie's done nothing but nag at him since the first day we met the poor boy!"

Trixie had been on the verge of telling them about the new black jacket, but Mart's dig made her change her mind. If her almost-twin felt that way about her, very well. She wouldn't tell him any of her ideas, no matter how important they were. Let him find out for himself!

She slapped the reins and sent her horse ahead of the others down the trail at a rapid pace.

"Wow! Somebody's feelings are hurt, I bet! You'd better go after her, Mart, and say you're sorry." Brian meant it.

"Let her run a couple of minutes and cool off," Mart grinned in the darkness. "She won't bite me then."

But Honey, flashing a reproachful look at the masculine members of the group, sent her own mount into a gallop and disappeared down the trail after Trixie.

When she had caught up with Trixie, who had wisely slowed down again once she was well out of sight of the boys, Honey scolded her for reckless riding in the darkness. "You might have gotten a broken neck."

"They wouldn't have cared," Trixie sulked, but she didn't mean it, and Honey knew that she didn't.

"I'm glad you left them behind, so we can talk," Trixie said quickly as they rode down the widening path toward Glen Road. "I want to tell you about the jacket."

"What was that all about, you and Dan yipping at each other in the cabin?" Honey asked curiously. "Why did you throw his silly jacket at him?"

"Because he looked so shocked when I touched it, there on the back of the chair! I guess he looked that way because he thought I'd noticed it wasn't the same one he's been wearing all along."

Honey looked astonished. "Not the same one? Why,

it must be. I'm sure he wouldn't have two. They're expensive. Don't you remember, when we were trying to decide what kind of jackets the Bob-Whites should have, we looked at leather ones in Brown's store."

"I remember," Trixie nodded. "But expensive or not, I still say this *wasn't* his same jacket. It was like it, but it had THE COWHANDS lettered across the back in white paint! And the left sleeve didn't have any sign of the tear that he got in his other jacket the day Susie brushed him off against the tree."

"Oh. . . ." Honey was beginning to be convinced. Then she frowned. "But where would he get the money for a new jacket?"

"He could have used the ten dollars he got for your watch from Mr. Lytell, for part of the cost. I hope I'm wrong, but if he *did* steal any of our racquets and stuff out of the clubhouse, he probably sold them to some of the kids at school."

"Do you think we should tell the boys about the new jacket? They could look around tomorrow and find out if anything's missing off the higher shelves where we keep the summer stuff."

"No." Trixie frowned. "Let's not tell them a thing till we're absolutely positive. They'd just tease us and talk the way Mart just did."

"I guess you're right," Honey admitted with a sigh. "Anyhow, if we tell them what we think about it, Mart might get into a fight with Dan and get hurt. Let's wait till Dan's been taken back to wherever he came from."

The boys caught up with them then, and they all rode on together to the lake.

Mart tried to apologize to his almost-twin, but she was cool and snubbed him until she noticed that he looked unhappy. Then she cooked him a special hamburger and decked it with his favorite trimmings as a token that she had forgiven him.

After that, they all had a good time, and while Mart practiced some fancy turns and twists out in the center of the ice, Trixie and Honey sped swiftly around at the edge arm in arm, and perfected a few spectacular tricks for the show.

As they rested out of the wind a few minutes, Honey noticed that Trixie was staring thoughtfully into the fire. "What's bothering you now?" Honey asked.

"Those yellow-brown cowboy boots that the thief wore who broke into our clubhouse. Dan couldn't have been wearing them. He'd have stumbled around and fallen over his own feet!"

"That's right," Honey agreed. Then she said, "But suppose he wore them just to confuse anybody who might suspect him!"

"He might have, at that," Trixie agreed.

"But where would he have gotten them? I never saw a pair for sale in Sleepyside!" Honey said, frowning.

"He could have stolen them, back wherever he came from!" Trixie decided. "He's told everybody in school how tough he is, and I guess he wasn't lying."

"I bet they're in a closet at Mr. Maypenny's right now!" Honey's eyes were wide with excitement.

"Maybe we can steal a look tomorrow, if we can wangle Moms into letting us ride out to see how Mr. Maypenny is getting along!" Trixie plotted eagerly.

It wasn't too much of a job next morning getting Mrs. Belden to agree. She thought the old gamekeeper might like some crabapple jelly, so she promised to pack a half dozen jars of it for Trixie to carry to him after school.

As the two girls were starting out to catch the school bus, the telephone rang. It was Miss Trask, and she wished to speak to Honey.

Honey danced back from the phone, her eyes sparkling. "Dad and Mother are flying in this afternoon, and I'm to meet them. Tom will pick me up at school!"

She was delighted. "They'll be here for the carnival. Isn't that wonderful?"

Trixie nodded, trying to be as happy about it as Honey, but it was a lost effort. She was going to miss her house guest, even though they saw each other every day.

Mrs. Belden zipped Bobby into his overcoat and put his hand in Trixie's, "Better run along ahead with him," she told Trixie. "His bus is almost due. I'll help Honey pack her things."

Bobby pulled away from Trixie's hand and ran to hug Honey. "Don't go away!" he pleaded. "I'll let you pet my new kitty when Trixie catches it for me!"

So Honey had to promise she would be back to share Trixie's room very soon and pet the kitty when it arrived. And only then did Bobby agree to run for the bus, hand in hand with Trixie.

It wasn't until they settled in their favorite seats on the next bus that Honey remembered their plan to go see Mr. Maypenny and do some private investigating. "Oh, dear! Now I won't be able to go with you!" she moaned.

"I know," Trixie said glumly. "I'll go by myself, and if I get a chance to snoop around and I find them," she promised, "I'll phone you the minute I get home!"

Regan wasn't around when she went to get Susie and saddle her, after school. The boys had gone to the lake in Brian's car with some more lumber odds and ends they were making into a little entrance booth where she could sit and hand out tickets in return for the schoolbooks that were to be the price of admission. Jim had already started another batch of posters, and he had also managed to salvage a lot of the others without too much repainting.

Susie was full of life and wanted to run in the brisk winter breeze, so Trixie arrived at the lake in a very short time. She had intended to do some more practicing with Honey, but now that it was impossible for that day, she took only a few turns around to convince her brothers that she was serious about it. Then she took off her skates and dropped them in the saddlebag next to Mr. Maypenny's jelly.

She led the beautiful young mare across to where the boys were erecting the ticket booth. "Guess I'll give Susie a good workout today," she told them casually. "Want me to drop by and see how Mr. Maypenny is getting along?"

Brian, his face grimy, and one thumb bandaged after a slight accident with a hammer, told her, "That's a genius idea, Sis. And if that Dan character isn't doing right by him, come back and tell us. I think if he tried real hard, your nuisance brother here could change the bandage for the old boy. I'm—" He held up the bandaged finger.

"—incapacitated physically," Mart finished the sentence. "And if I couldn't put on a neater bandage than the one you hung on Mr. Maypenny last night, I'd go in for boilermaking instead of surgery!" He ducked behind the booth with a grin, as Brian grabbed up a plank and threatened him playfully with it.

"Hey, quit clowning, clowns!" Jim called from the lumber pile. "And help me carry some planks!"

While they were doing it, Trixie mounted and turned Susie's nose in the direction of the uphill trail that led to Mr. Maypenny's cabin.

She rode through the snow-prettied woods, under a clear pale blue winter sky, and thought how good it was to have a fine horse to ride—even if Susie wasn't really her own personal property. She was *practically* her own, because the Wheelers had bought the little mare so Trixie could ride with Honey.

She wasn't paying much attention to where she was along the trail. Susie was beginning to slow down a little as she got some of the friskiness out of her system in the uphill climb, when suddenly, Trixie recognized a familiar spot. Under the tall evergreens at the meeting of two trails, the snow on the ground was trampled by many feet. Several evergreen branches lay around, evidently broken off by the heavy wind. This was where Mr. Maypenny had been struck by the falling branch last night.

On an impulse she stopped the mare and slid out of the saddle. "Take it easy a few minutes, girl," she told Susie, stroking her soft nose. "We still have a mile to go, and a steep one at that."

She looped Susie's bridle around a sapling beside the trail and wandered over to look around and to stretch her legs. She wondered idly which branch had fallen on poor Mr. Maypenny.

There was a small branch lying at one side. It was only about twenty inches long, and someone had cut all the side twigs off it. It looked more like a length of trimmed firewood than a fallen branch.

Trixie picked it up, curious as usual. She was surprised to see that it wasn't a branch of the evergreen that towered overhead. It came from a crabapple tree.

"That's funny," she told herself. "I don't see a crabapple tree anywhere around here. Somebody must have brought this here to whittle on."

But just as she decided that, she noticed for the first time that there was a dark stain at the heavy end of the piece of wood. And caught in the grain of the wood was a small tuft of gray hair. Hair like the hair on Mr. Maypenny's head!

The stain could only be his blood! And it was this homemade weapon that had struck him down, not a branch of the evergreen, laden with snow!

Chapter 17
Runaway Dan

For a minute or two, all Trixie could do was stare in horrified surprise at the telltale length of crabapple branch in her hands. Then, as the full meaning of it came to her, she started to fling it away, shivering. She stopped with the club poised to throw.

Someone had struck down poor Mr. Maypenny last night with this, probably as he was looking around for Dan to tell him the good news that the kids had found evidence that seemed to clear Dan. Someone had sneaked up on the old gamekeeper from behind. And he didn't suspect it. He blamed a falling branch.

It could happen again to him, if he weren't warned. And it seemed that she had to be the one to warn him, because no one else had noticed the broken length of branch with its ugly stain.

She looked around her with a shudder. At any moment, Mr. Maypenny's attacker might show himself, and see that she had guessed the truth. He might strike at *her*.

She ran for her horse and scrambled up into the

saddle. It wasn't far to Mr. Maypenny's house, and if anyone tried to stop her, she would hit him with the length of wood and ride on. "Come on, Susie pie! Let's go!" She gave the reluctant Susie a little kick with her heels, and the indignant young mare set out with a leap and carried her up the trail.

But she hadn't gone over a hundred yards when she saw a figure approaching mounted on a sturdy old horse which she recognized moments before she guessed who was riding it. It was Mr. Maypenny's old Brownie, the ancient mare who never moved faster than a dignified walk that matched her fifteen years of age. And the figure on her back was Mr. Maypenny himself, his head neatly bandaged.

"Oh, Mr. Maypenny! I'm so glad you are all right!" she called. She dismounted and waited for him.

"Well, now, I wouldn't say that exactly," Mr. Maypenny corrected her, lifting a hand to touch the bandage rather gingerly. "Still got an almighty nuisance of a headache to plague me. What you doin' out here alone? That catamount's been yowlin' again up in the hills."

"I won't hang around out here long," Trixie told him, after a nervous glance around. "I was coming to tell you something."

"Well, tell away, Sis, and then you skedaddle for home," he said severely.

So Trixie, showing him the crabapple branch with its telltale stain, told him she had found it at the place where he thought a branch had fallen on him.

She was puzzled when he didn't show any surprise at the information. He reached for the length of wood, regarded it gravely a moment, and then dropped it into his saddlebag.

"Thanks, youngster. I had a notion maybe it wasn't an accident. I'm missing my wallet and the five dollars that was in it. I was comin' to look around the ground back there to see if maybe it fell out of my pocket."

"There's no sign of it, Mr. Maypenny," Trixie told him.

"Guess I won't waste my time after all," he said with a sigh. "But I was hopin' against hope it'd be there and the money still in it. Guess I knew better all along."

"Maybe Dan has seen the tramp or whoever it was that did it! Did you ask him if there's been anybody around?" Trixie asked quickly.

Mr. Maypenny shook his head slowly. "Thought I might ask him this morning, but when I got up, he was gone."

"He wasn't at school," Trixie said, frowning. "I

guess he decided to work all day in the preserve, as long as you wouldn't feel well enough to get around."

"I kinda hoped that's where he was, but when I went out to the barn to see if he took old Spartan, the horse was still there. And I found this." He handed Trixie a torn sheet of paper.

There were only a few words scribbled in pencil on it. "I won't be back. Don't look for me. Dan." And down in one corner, in small letters, as if in an afterthought, he had written, "Thanks."

Trixie stared at it without speaking for a long moment. Then she handed the note back to Mr. Maypenny. He tucked it into the pocket of his high-necked old-fashioned sweater. "Looks like he's run away, doesn't it?" Mr. Maypenny said with a sigh. "Poor little lad!"

Trixie nodded sympathetically. "It's a shame, Mr. Maypenny. He *is* your grandson, isn't he?"

"Nope. Dan's no kin of mine. I let him work here to oblige a friend of mine."

"Do you mean Regan?" Trixie asked him, point-blank.

The old man hesitated. Then he said with a shrug, "Can't see why we should keep it quiet any longer, now the boy's gone. Regan's the one."

"But why was it such a big mystery?" Trixie frowned. "And what relation is he to Regan?"

"Dan's mother was Regan's only sister. They were raised together in the orphanage, and she ran off to get married. Tim Mangan was killed in Korea and she had the boy to raise alone. Regan never knew where she was till the day he got word that his sister was dead and her boy was in a street gang fight and headed for reform school."

"So he asked Moms and Miss Trask what to do—!" Trixie supplied quickly.

"That's right. Judge said he'd give the lad a chance to straighten out, if Regan would give him a home and work, so—" he paused, with a sigh, "we tried your mom's idea that working out in the preserve would do him good, give him a slant on other things than gangs and fighting."

"But why couldn't he work at Wheelers' helping in the stables, instead?" Trixie knitted her brows.

"Regan figured Mr. Wheeler might not like the idea of having a boy like that around with *his* youngsters."

"I don't know," Trixie thought it over. "Maybe Mrs. Wheeler might have felt sort of funny about it, but I should think Mr. Wheeler would know Honey and Jim better than to think Dan could have made them do anything wrong."

"I guess poor Regan leaned back a little, at that," Mr. Maypenny admitted with a solemn shake of his head. "But it's better to be safe than sorry, I say. And look how the boy's acted!"

Trixie frowned. "All he's done is run away, and maybe he didn't want to do that!"

"You're forgetting Honey's watch he found and sold," Mr. Maypenny reminded her. He put his hand to the bandage on his head. "And other things that have happened."

"Maybe he didn't do all of them," Trixie said quietly. "Have you seen anybody around lately wearing those silly cowboy boots like Dan's, only *brown* ones instead of black?"

"Can't say I have. What's on your mind?" he said with surprise.

Trixie reminded him of the brown polish on the clubhouse table and the large size bootmarks. Then she told him about the almost new black jacket she had seen and Dan had tried to conceal.

Through the recital, old Mr. Maypenny stared at her, doubtfully at first, then with growing excitement. He interrupted her as she was telling about hearing a step up in the attic of the cabin last night.

"That's it! I know I heard a strange voice while I

was lying there! I thought I was dreamin' it, on account of the bump I got on my head, but I guess it was real."

"What did you hear?" Trixie asked eagerly.

The gamekeeper thought it over. "Kind of an argument, it seemed like. I was pretty dizzy, and part of the time I guess I was out, but every now an' then, I'd come to, and hear the voices, Dan's and somebody else's."

"Did you hear what they were saying?" she asked, her blue eyes sparkling with the excitement of the mystery.

"Not much," he admitted. "I recollect that the other one was laughing and poking fun at Dan—" He shook his head. "—Seems like he was calling him 'yeller' in a mean kind of voice, and I heard Dan say, 'I won't do it.' "

Trixie waited for him to go on, and when he didn't, she urged, "What else, Mr. Maypenny?"

The old man shrugged his shoulders. "That's about all I remember. Drifted off again, about that time."

Trixie was disappointed. Then she began her maybe-ing.

"Maybe he wanted to make Dan run away, and Dan didn't want to go. Maybe the other one had a gun and just *made* him come along!" She was building up the scene in her mind. "Maybe they struggled, and he

210

knocked Dan out—*pow!* And then he dragged Dan away with him—"

"And maybe it didn't happen that way at all," he interrupted wearily. "All I know is, when Regan gets back from the city, I'm giving him the books and things the young one left behind him, and then I'm washing my hands of the whole thing. And nobody can blame me!" He touched the bandage again and winced at the touch. "I guess we all expected too much of a wild kid. He's better off in reform school."

Trixie felt sad. Dan and she hadn't hit it off well, but maybe, as Jim had told the Bob-Whites a couple of times, people don't feel very friendly to others after being arrested and all. "Jim's told us how awful it is not to have a good home and people around who care about what becomes of you," she told Mr. Maypenny gravely. "He always says he was just lucky he didn't get in with the wrong bunch himself and get into trouble. I guess Dan wasn't so lucky."

"Guess not, young one. And you better be getting back to the lake and starting for home. Sun's low and you oughtn't to be out in the woods in the dark."

"I'm on my way right now," Trixie assured him. "I'll tell Brian your head is just fine," she called to the old man as she swung into Susie's saddle and headed the young mare back toward the lake. "Hope you like the jelly. Moms makes oodles of it every fall and she's won heaps of blue ribbons for it at the county fair."

"Tell her, 'Much obliged,' " he called after her as she rode down the trail.

She was surprised as she rode down the hill to the lake, to find that the boys had finished work on the rows of plank seats they had been building and were gone.

They had stamped out the fire before they left, and there was a cold wind blowing in heavy gusts across the ice. But there was a beautiful sunset, with scurrying pink and crimson clouds, and the ice looked so inviting that she took her skates out of her saddlebag and put them on to try it.

It was fun skating around in a pink glow as if she were on a vast stage in a colored spotlight. She sped around the edge of the lake and then out into the middle and did a fancy twirl, a leap, and a spectacular finish that ended in a bow to her imaginary audience in the empty rows of benches.

But as she glided off the ice, something moved among the trees a hundred feet away and caught her eye. She stopped to stare, half blinded by the level rays of the red ball of sun. She saw two figures hurrying away over the hill. One was short and the other was

somewhat taller. And they both were wearing black leather jackets and caps.

Now she knew. Dan the runaway was not alone. He was with the other one whose voice Mr. Maypenny had heard, and whose black jacket she had seen and touched on the back of the chair in the Maypenny cabin!

They had been watching her while she skated. Her face flushed as she thought how silly she must have seemed to them as she took a bow before the imaginary audience. It was most annoying.

She removed her skates, frowning all the time, and plunked them back into the saddlebag. "Come on, Susie, let's go home. The free show's over!" She mounted and turned Susie's nose in the direction of the homeward trail.

The red sun had dipped below the hills, and the twilight shadows were deep all around. Strange noises came from the woods nearby. She knew they were only natural forest sounds, but at that spooky time of night, she was jumpy and expected every minute that Dan Mangan and his unknown friend would reappear. And she didn't want to meet them.

She urged the little mare on down the trail, but Susie was being stubborn. She would go only so fast, and her ears twitched nervously at every small sound.

Suddenly something small and furry darted across the path almost at Susie's feet. After it came another, this one unmistakably a fox. It disappeared into the brush and rocks as Susie, neighing with fright, reared and dropped Trixie out of the saddle.

She landed in a drift of deep snow beside the path and scrambled to her feet in time to see Susie running back up the path the way they had just come.

"Susie! Whoa, girl! Whoa!" she called out, and ran after her along the darkening trail as fast as she could.

But the nervous young mare veered off the trail and crashed through the bushes in a wild, cross-country run, her reins flying loose behind her.

And in a couple of minutes she had disappeared into the depths of the wild bit of forest that they called the labyrinth because it had no regular trails and was still as wild as it had been when the first settlers came to the valley long years ago.

Chapter 18
Double Danger!

Trixie went as fast as she could along the dark trail, calling, "Whoa, Susie!" in tones that got weaker and weaker as she became more breathless. There was no sight or sound of the runaway mare now. She had disappeared in the blackness of the deep woods.

Trixie stumbled to the side of the trail and sank onto the nearest flat boulder. She didn't even look to see if she was sitting on a rock or a pile of snow, she was so tired and hopeless.

The trees met over her head and the sky was a dull gray, all the more depressing when she realized that in a very few minutes it would be dark, scary night.

She hadn't the slightest idea where she was. The moon wouldn't be rising for a long time yet, and only a faint glow in what must have been the west gave her an idea of where home would be if she could ever get there.

It was awfully quiet in the deep woods. Even the crack of a twig as some little kangaroo mouse hopped through the underbrush sounded loud and menacing.

Trixie stood up and cupped her hands around her mouth. "Halloo! Halloo!" she called. But the only answer she got was an echo of her own voice, followed by a myriad of small sounds from the scampering citizens of the woods whom she had disturbed.

Well, that's that, she thought, swallowing hard. *I guess I'd better stay right here. I'm sure when they miss me at home, they'll come out and look for me. Maybe Susie is there already. She's always hungry for her supper, so I guess she'll run home as straight as she can!*

It was a comforting thought and kept her cheerful for at least two minutes, while she was picturing to herself how she would meet her rescuers. She would be tired but, oh, awfully brave! She would smile and say, "You needn't have worried about me. I could have found my way home easily in the morning. The dark? Oh, I don't mind the dark. I know there's nothing to hurt me—" And even Mart would say, "Trix, you're a brave girl!"

But when she had pictured that unlikely scene, a sudden gust of biting wind through the tops of the tall trees made a weird screeching noise, and she covered her face with her hands and cowered down on the rock.

Then, just as she was reasoning out the cause of that, she heard a new sound that was even more scary, like a child calling, "Mommy! Mommy!" in a wailing cry.

It wasn't like the yowl of the catamount she and Honey had heard. It was more human. And as she stood rigidly listening, she heard it again. "Mommy! I want Mommy!" it sobbed in an all-too-familiar voice.

Bobby! she thought, horrified. *But it can't be!* She looked all around at the darkness as the cries went on.

"Bobby! Where are you, darling? It's Trixie! Bobby, answer me right away! Where are you?"

"Trixie?" the voice faltered. "Is 'at you, Trixie?"

"Coming, Bobby! Just sing out real loud, so I can tell where you are! That's my lamb!" Trixie called cheerfully. She had caught an inkling of which direction the last call had come from, and she hurried toward it.

There was a steep hill, and a yawning hole showed itself as she came around a group of rocks. The voice was coming from the cavelike hole. "Trixie? Don't go away!" There was a hysterical note in the small voice now.

Trixie plunged recklessly into the hole. "Bobby! Here I am! Come on out and say hello!"

But he answered, with a sob, "I c-can't! It's holding me!"

She was well inside the cave now, and groping about, hoping to contact her small brother. "I'm stuck!" The voice came surprisingly from below, and Trixie realized with a shock that she had almost stumbled into a deep hole.

Somewhere down that hole, Bobby was "stuck." She felt panic, but she knew she couldn't give way to it without terrifying Bobby as well. She forced herself to keep her voice calm, as she called down to him, "It's all right, honey. I'll come down and get you right away."

"Hurry up, Trixie," Bobby's voice came crossly. "I'm hungry and it's dark down here, and the rock is holding my legs."

"Coming right now!" she assured him with make-believe cheerfulness. Then she let herself over the edge of the hole in the floor of the cave. "I'm climbing down. Look out below!" She made herself laugh to cheer him.

Now she was at the bottom of the hole, and she felt around in the darkness for Bobby. Instead of the curly head she expected to touch, she found only another and much narrower opening than the one in the floor of the cave through which she had let herself down. And Bobby's voice, now a little thin and tired, complained from inside that hole, "I'm gettin' sleepy, Trixie. Please pull me out!"

She knelt on the soft dirt floor and reached into the hole. It was rock-lined, and far too narrow for her to enter, but by stretching as far as she could reach into the hole, she could touch Bobby's hand as it reached out to meet hers.

She reached in as far as she could and took his small wrist in a firm grip. "Okay, skipper, here we go! I'll pull and you wiggle this way and we'll get you out in a second! Hang on to my wrist now!"

"Awright," he answered. And when she pulled at his arm, she heard him grunt and felt his fingers dig into her wrist. He was trying hard. Then suddenly his wrist went limp and his fingers let go. "The rock won't let me go," he complained with a sob. "It's holding me!"

"Bobby," she tried to keep the fear out of her voice, "does it hurt a lot when you try to get away?"

"No." Bobby's voice sounded weary now. "I feel fine but I'm hungry an' you better pull me out, right now."

A cold chill ran through her. If he didn't feel any pain, it could mean the rock had injured his spine. Pulling and tugging at him could only make the damage worse.

Somehow, somewhere, she would have to find help! But where? She was lost. She hadn't the slightest idea which direction to go to find anyone. But she had to try.

"Bobby, honey," she said, patting the small hand

that now lay limp, outstretched, "your silly old Trixie has to go find Jim and Mart and Brian so they can move the mean old rock that's holding you. Will you stay real quiet for a little while? Maybe you'd better put your head down now and rest till I get back." She tried to sound cheerful and unworried.

There was a little pause, and she heard the sound of a yawn. Then, "Awright, but when you pull me out will you help me find the kitty? It was a nice big one, and it runned when I tried to catch it, and I thought it was in the cave, and I fell in the hole, and—" The voice had grown fainter. Now it stopped.

"Gleeps!" Trixie said to herself. "I better find somebody in a hurry. I hope he stays asleep."

She wriggled clear of the narrow opening beyond which he was trapped and stood up in the hole in the cave floor. It wasn't as easy to get out of it as it had been to drop down into it, but she managed, in her desperation, to claw her way up into the cave and stumble out into the starlit night.

If I only knew which way to go! she thought, staring all around her despairingly. The wind was starting to blow now, and overhead big masses of clouds tumbled through the sky. She slapped her arms across her chest to warm herself a little. But her teeth chattered as much from a very real fear as they did from the cold, the fear that before help could come for Bobby, he could freeze down there under the chilly earth.

Two large tears rolled down her cheeks, but she dashed them away angrily. "Trixie Belden! Crying isn't going to help any. Think of something! Think!" But her mind seemed to be numbed.

Then, as for the sixteenth time she turned slowly, searching the darkness for some sign of where she was, she saw against the inky darkness the flickering of a distant campfire. The bushes that had stood between her and the welcome sight were being whipped about by the wind, or she wouldn't have caught even that small glimpse of the little fire.

She cupped her hands around her mouth and hallooed, but even as she was doing it, she knew it was useless. The wind was carrying the sound away.

There was no choice. She had to get to that campfire and bring help for Bobby. She took a few steps, almost sobbing with relief.

But she came to a sudden stop before she had gone two yards. How would she get back to this dark place? She could see no landmarks to remember, and the trees around looked like a thousand other trees in the labyrinth. Suppose she went to the campfire for help and couldn't get back to Bobby again. It was too big a risk.

She couldn't just stay there. There had to be an answer!

Suddenly it came to her. Her white wool sweater! Aunt Alicia had knitted it on big wooden needles so it would be fashionably bulky. It would unravel easily.

She pulled it off over her head and tore apart the big stitches of the bottom border. Once she had found the right stitch to pull, the rest was easy. The sweater unraveled with miraculous speed.

She tied the end of the white wool to the bush that grew beside the cave entrance and started toward the distant fire, letting the sweater unravel as she went.

In and out, down ravines and up again, between trees and around rocks, Trixie went grimly on. When the woolen yarn gave out at a knot, she tied it again and went on, and always there was an unbroken string of white between her and the cave.

Then, at last, she came to the final barrier of wind-tossed bushes and shoved her way through to stand on the edge of the clearing where, only a hundred feet away, the small fire burned brightly and there was a smell of cooking meat on the air.

She stumbled forward with a word of greeting on her lips, almost hysterical with relief. But before the two who sat beside the fire could glance her way, she stopped dead, the greeting unspoken.

The two at the fire were runaway Dan Mangan and another older boy in a black jacket. While she stood rooted to the spot, staring unhappily at them, the other boy rose and went to the fire to help himself to whatever it was they were cooking.

He was tall and she saw by the firelight that he was dark and sharp-faced and seemed a few years older than Dan.

Would they help her rescue Bobby? Or would they refuse and sneer at her for her helplessness? Dan might still be angry and hurt at the way she had acted toward him. *But if I tell him I know he didn't steal our temper money and didn't hurt Mr. Maypenny, then I'd have to say I thought it was the other one with him who had done it! And* he'd *refuse to help Bobby or let Dan help!*

Chapter 19
Rescue

Trixie crouched in the darkness and watched the two figures at the campfire. She was blue with cold, and the thought of Bobby trapped in the hole in the mountain was making her desperate. But what could she expect from them?

She could see that they were quarreling. The tall, broad-shouldered boy stood over Dan Mangan and said something angrily. She could see Dan look startled and sullen, but he shook his head as if he were refusing something.

Now the tall one was picking up a canvas knapsack and slinging it over his shoulder. He was getting ready to leave. But Dan just sat where he was, staring at him and shaking his head.

Trixie darted to the shelter of a pile of granite rocks only ten or twelve feet from the two boys. The moment that the tall boy left, she intended to rush to Dan Mangan and ask him to help rescue Bobby.

The wind carried their voices to her as she crouched there, shivering.

"A guy can change his mind about things, can't he?" Dan protested defiantly.

"Yeah, if he's too yeller to take a chance!" the tall one sneered. "Your letter said there'd be good pickin's at the Wheeler joint and you'd show me the ropes so we could get in an' out again without any trouble. Now you're backin' down!"

Dan was on his feet now, and seemed a little uncertain. "But, Luke! They're not like I thought they were. They're real regular, and so's old man Maypenny."

"You're just yeller," Luke insisted with a sneer. "You've got it soft here and your real friends don't mean a thing to you any more. I oughta give you a beatin'!"

Trixie could see that Dan was afraid of the bigger boy. He stepped back a little as if he were expecting Luke to start hitting him at any moment.

"Come on! I oughta leave you here, but I'll give you one last chance. Are you comin' with me or are you hangin' around the backwoods some more?"

"Aw, don't rush me. I'm thinkin' it over," Dan said uneasily. "Anyhow, why can't we just get out of here and head back to the city? We can figure out plenty of ways to get more money there than you can get breakin' into Wheelers'. How about it, Luke? Let's call off the action and pull out!"

"Go ahead and welsh out, bud," Luke said with a nasty laugh that made Trixie shudder. "But I'll still go ahead the way we talked it over when your uncle was coming to get you from the court."

Even in the flickering light of the small fire, Trixie could see the expression of relief that came to Dan's face at Luke's words. "No hard feelings, Luke?"

"Nah, kid!" Luke chuckled. "Only, if I get nabbed by the cops, I'll tell 'em you're in on it, too. And I'll tell 'em you clobbered old Maypenny and swiped his wallet."

"They won't believe you! I wasn't near the place! I didn't know you were going to do it!"

"Who's goin' to believe you, kid? Not the cops, not your Uncle Regan! Better change your mind and come along!" Luke laughed and picked up a small suitcase that had been sitting a few feet from the fire. "Here!"

Dan caught the small bag and stood holding it as Luke started to gather his own things.

Trixie felt her heart sink. And then, as she tried to summon the courage to stop them and ask for help, she heard the eerie howl of the catamount just as she and Honey had heard it days before. And to her worried brain, it sounded as if it might be coming from the direction of the cave where Bobby was trapped and helpless. What if—if that had been its hiding place?

Everything else was forgotten. She came out from behind the rock as Luke and Dan were turning away from the flickering fire.

"Dan! You've got to help me! Bobby's caught in a hole and I can't pull him out!" She stumbled and fell to her knees and burst out crying.

Dan stopped, staring in amazement, and then, dropping his bag, he ran to her, while Luke stood watching with a scowl.

"Trixie!" Dan helped her to her feet. "What's the idea of being way out here after dark? Don't you have any brains?"

"Trixie, hey?" Luke cut in before Trixie could start to explain. "So that's the snooper! Come on, leave her there. She's cooked up a story again, like you said she was always doin'. She don't need any help. She's probably tryin' to stall us here so her snooty friends can catch you for Regan!"

"I'm not!" Trixie glared at him through her tears. "Dan, you've got to believe me! Bobby's stuck in a cave, and—" In the distance the catamount howled again and she broke off with a little cry of despair. "If you don't come and help him, that awful thing may get him!"

"The poor little guy!" Dan said. "Where is he? How far is it?"

"I'll show you, but hurry!" Trixie pulled at his jacket sleeve. "Please!"

Dan looked apologetically at Luke. "Won't take long. I'll be right back. He's only a six-year-old kid!"

"And you're a fool, Dan Mangan, if you think I'm hangin' around any longer. Stay here with your friends, but don't forget, if anything happens where I'm going, you're in it deep!"

With the last words, Luke turned and strode out of sight into the darkness of the woods.

For a minute, Dan stared after him uncertainly. But Trixie pulled at his sleeve. "Please, Dan! We *are* your friends, really. Don't mind him! Come and help Bobby, please!"

"Okay, okay!" Dan said. "Which way? And we better hurry. That cat sounded nearer this time!"

Trixie looked about quickly for the remains of the white wool sweater that she had dropped as she came out through the bushes into the clearing. It was still lying on the ground in front of the bushes, and the newly risen moon was shining clearly on it. "There! That's the way!" She started toward it.

"Wait a minute!" Dan called, and when she looked

back impatiently, she saw him taking off the black leather jacket hastily and coming toward her with it. "Here, get into this! I won't need it!"

"But you'll be cold!" She protested, but she didn't resist as Dan helped her into it.

"Not if we move fast," he assured her. "Besides, I can take it better than a girl."

Trixie couldn't help smiling to herself in the darkness as they started following the white woolen string back toward Bobby. *I guess all boys are like Mart and think they're smarter and stronger than girls,* she thought, and let him lead the way with his flashlight, though she felt that she really could have gone faster if *she* had led.

They were soon at the mouth of the cave and Trixie called out softly as they went into it, "Bobby, honey, are you awake?" while Dan played the flashlight around and then centered it on the gaping hole in the floor.

Trixie ran forward and knelt at the edge. "Bobby," she called uncertainly, "are you asleep?"

There was no answer. But neither were there any catamount tracks visible in the soft dirt of the cave floor. She breathed more freely as she saw that.

"Better let me get down," Dan advised. "He's probably fast asleep, so don't try to wake him up till I get a chance to see the lay of the land and find out what's holding him."

"A rock, he said," Trixie answered, swallowing a lump in her throat that made her voice tremble.

"Might be just some earth," Dan said quickly. "Quit getting hysterical! Girls make me sick!" And with that he let himself and his flashlight down into the hole.

"I'm sorry," Trixie admitted in a small but firmer voice. "Tell me what to do to help and I'll do it."

There was a momentary silence and she saw the reflected beam of the flashlight moving around down there. Then, to her infinite relief, she heard Bobby's voice as it said sleepily, "Hello, mister. Did you falled down the hole, too?"

And Dan's answering cheerfully, "Sure did, boy! But we're going to climb out real quick, aren't we?"

"Uh-huh," Bobby's voice agreed. "Where's Trixie? She runned away."

"I'm right here, Bobby!" Trixie called down to him as cheerfully as she could manage. "And this is Danny Mangan, honey, who's come to get you out of that mean old hole!"

"Tha's good!" Bobby's voice said a little faintly. "But hurry. I'm hungry."

"Be right back, Bobby," Dan told him. "I've got to get something."

"Awright," Bobby said and then was silent.

Dan stood on tiptoe in the hole and beckoned Trixie over to the edge. She leaned down as he whispered, "Here, take these matches and get a fire started. As big a one as you can, so somebody'll be sure to see it! The air down there is getting bad, and I don't know how long it's going to take to chip away the rock that's holding Bobby's legs."

"But you don't have anything to chip it with!" Trixie moaned. "What are you going to do?"

"Use this." Dan held up a stubby-looking pocket-knife and flicked open the long blade with a touch of his thumb. "Luke just gave it to me. He brought it for me to use when we held up the Wheelers."

"Oh!" Trixie stared at it fascinated. "What a horrible-looking thing! Is that what you call a switch blade?"

"Yeah! And I darn near wouldn't take it! Boy, am I glad now I did!" He ducked down again and left her in darkness.

A moment later, as she still crouched there feeling a little sick at the thought of what might be happening at the Wheelers' tonight after Luke broke in, she heard Dan start to chip away at the rock.

"Say, this isn't as hard as it looked," she heard him tell Bobby cheerfully. "Got another big hunk loose. You just stay flat there, sonny, and we'll have you out before you can say:

'Tip-tap, rip-rap,
Ticka tack too!
This way, that way,
So we make a shoe!'

"That's what the fairy shoemaker sings, my mother told me!" And the chipping continued steadily.

"Tip-tap, rip-rap," she heard Bobby repeat sleepily. "Say it again!" He wasn't afraid now. He loved rhymes.

She moved back from the rim of the hole and hurried outside with the matches. There were plenty of small dry twigs lying around, and within a couple of minutes she had gathered them and started a brisk little fire.

Soon it was blazing high enough to be seen for a mile at least against the night sky. And as she turned her back to it and looked around, she saw flashes of white light far off in the direction she had gone to the campfire where she had found the two boys.

Although she knew it was dangerous to have too

big a fire in the woods, even though they were thoroughly soaked from rain and snow, she heaped twigs and branches on it. Soon smoke was rising high into the sky in a thick column and the wind was whipping it toward the flashing white lights that she knew must be electric torches in the hands of a search party.

Now they seemed to be coming closer. They were probably shouting her name and Bobby's. She couldn't hear them with the wind against them, and she was afraid of frightening Bobby if she yelled, "Help!" So all she could do was wait and hope, and feed the high-leaping flames.

She went into the cave and listened. The chipping sound was still going on. Bobby wasn't free yet.

She leaned down into the hole in the cave floor. She couldn't see Dan's feet now. He must have had to crawl deeper into the narrower hole.

Then the chipping sound stopped, and she heard Dan's voice. "Looks like we've got it, bud. Let's see you make believe you're a little frog. Wiggle your legs and scrunch along on your tummy!"

Trixie held her breath. There was a scraping sound and a little giggle from Bobby. "Gunk! Grunk!" he said, in what he hoped was acceptable frog language, and Dan laughed, "Hi, froggy! Come on out!"

His legs were all right, the rock hadn't hurt his spine! Trixie was almost dizzy with relief.

She leaned down into the hole as Dan stood aside and they watched Bobby wriggle out of the narrow opening in the rocky earth. He was grimy and his face, where tears had streaked it, was muddy, but he stood up straight with Dan's help, and looked up at Trixie.

"When are we going home?" he demanded. "I'm hungry!"

Trixie reached for him as Dan lifted him and handed him up to her.

"Darling!" She hugged him hard till he managed to break loose.

"Thanks, so much!" Trixie smiled at Dan as he climbed up out of the hole. She thrust out her hand impulsively. "Friend?"

Dan hesitated and then took her hand. "Okay, friend." Then he dropped her hand and stepped back, with a frown. "You'd better keep that fire going outside, so your friends can find you. I think I'll get going."

Trixie regarded him soberly. "I wish you could stick around. Dad will want to say thanks, and so will Moms and the boys."

But Dan shook his head firmly. "I don't belong around here. My uncle's taking me back to the city at the end of the week. I guess that's the right place for me."

They had reached the mouth of the cave. The leaping flames were high, and the light on their faces showed Dan's unhappiness and Trixie's regret.

"I suppose you know what's best, but we'd all like you to stay in Sleepyside. We have lots of fun, and I know you would, too."

Dan's face was sober. He nodded. "Yeah, I guess I might. But I don't think some people would want me around when it gets out about Luke and all."

"Nonsense!" It was the old Trixie, spunky and sure of herself. "If they don't—"

"Trixie!" Bobby ran up and grabbed her arm. "My shoe! My shoe's down there! Get it for me!"

Chapter 20
Thanks to Dan Mangan

"I losted my shoe an' my foot's c-c-cold!" Bobby insisted, clinging to his sister's sleeve. "Please, Trixie, get it for me. It's down in the hole."

"But, Bobby—" Trixie didn't want to go into that cave again for anything.

"I want my shoe!" Bobby wailed, suddenly bursting into tears.

"Oh, all right!" she agreed. "Here, Dan." She took off the black leather jacket and held it out to him. "You better wear this yourself now."

He took it rather reluctantly, and she noticed by the light of the leaping flames of her bonfire that the tear in the sleeve was still unmended. "Thanks, guess I'll be on my way. Maybe I can catch up with Luke and talk him out of going to the Wheelers'. Be seeing you sometime." He slipped his arms into the jacket and started to go. But he hadn't gone beyond the circle of firelight before there was an eerie screech from the catamount, somewhere not very far off.

"Please don't go! I'm scared!" Trixie called, throwing her arms around Bobby and holding him tight, and turning a pleading look toward Dan.

Dan hesitated and then came back. "Okay, I'll stay till we're sure your search party's close." He drew the switch-blade knife and snapped it open as he stood facing the direction that the big cat's cry seemed to have come from.

Another yowl was closer, and Bobby buried his face against his sister's skirt. "Let's go home!" he demanded tearfully. "I don' like it here!"

Now they could hear the shouts of the approaching party. "Trixie!" That was her father calling. "Bobby!"

Trixie tried to answer, but her throat seemed paralyzed. She held tight to Bobby, staring into the darkness. "C-Can you see any yellow eyes?" she asked Dan fearfully.

"Nah," Dan assured her, but he still held the knife ready in his hand, and his voice shook a little. "It won't come here as long as you keep the fire going."

The words were no sooner out of Dan's mouth than the mountain lion yowled again, now unmistakably only a short distance off. But this time the awful screech broke off suddenly as a rifle shot blasted deafeningly somewhere out in the darkness.

Then for a moment there was complete silence, and the three of them stood frozen, waiting.

A sudden crashing in the underbrush made Dan's hand tighten on the knife-handle, and he placed himself quickly between Trixie and Bobby and the spot from which the sound was coming. At any moment both he and Trixie expected the great cat to come bounding in at them.

Instead, it was Bill Regan who shoved his way through the bushes toward them, rifle in hand.

"Trixie!" he was shouting. "Bobby!" Then he saw Dan, knife in hand, apparently barring his way to the two who were clinging together behind him. "Drop it, Dan!" the big man called out harshly. "Don't try to use it!"

Dan stood staring at him in stunned surprise. Regan stalked to him and snatched the knife out of his hand. Dan was bewildered and made no resistance as Regan gripped him by the arm and called back to the others who were crashing through the brush after him. "They're okay, Mr. Belden!"

As her father and brothers ran in, Trixie shouted at Regan. "He wasn't trying to do anything wrong! He was only trying to protect us from that horrible wildcat!"

Regan looked astonished and turned abruptly to Dan. "Is that the truth, Dan? Out with it!"

Dan shrugged his thin shoulders, and a bitter little

smile twisted his mouth. "What did you think I was doing? Holding them for a kidnap payoff or something?" He was the old Dan now, sarcastic and on the defensive.

Regan still looked doubtful, and the others were staring at the pair. Trixie could see that none of them was quite ready to believe Dan's real role.

Brian brought her a cup of hot broth from his Thermos bottle, but she waved it aside. "Dan needs that more than I do," she said. "He came right away when I asked him to help us, and he made me wear his jacket so I wouldn't get cold while he was crawling down into that horrible hole to save Bobby from freezing to death with his legs caught under a rock!" It was a long speech, but it had the effect that she hoped it would. Everyone was looking at Dan now with admiration, and Brian was handing him the cup of broth.

"Thanks, Dan," Mr. Belden said quietly, holding Bobby tightly in his arms. "We won't forget it!"

Dan seemed embarrassed by their approval. He didn't know what to say so he started sipping the hot broth.

Bobby lifted his head as Mart draped a blanket around him in his father's arms. "I falled in a hole but the kitty wasn't there. An' Dan digged me out, an' there was a fairy shoemaker an' he said—" A big yawn interrupted the story, and he ended sleepily, "Tip-tap, rip-rap—" And a moment later he was sound asleep.

"It was just a little rhyme," Dan apologized, "about a leprechaun. My mum used to sing it to me."

"A leprechaun!" Trixie clapped her hands. "I know what we'll do! We need something special for the carnival! We'll have Dan recite the rhyme, and Bobby will do his little skating number dressed in a leprechaun costume! Honey can make it in nothing flat!"

"Sounds like a swell idea!" Mart agreed with his almost-twin, much to her surprise. Usually, he found a lot of objections to all her suggestions and had to be convinced one by one.

"Danny's a good skater, aren't you, boy?" Bill Regan asked him. "Didn't I hear you won a medal in the Police Athletic League games a couple of years ago?"

"Yeah." Dan was embarrassed again. "But I haven't skated for a long time."

"That's easy to take care of," Trixie said eagerly. "We still have a few days before Saturday and the carnival, and you can practice like mad. We're all going to, and if you don't have your skates with you, you can use Mart's or Brian's old ones. We can sharpen them up for you!"

"Needn't bother, Trixie," Regan said, putting his

arm across Dan's shoulders. "I'll pick up a pair for my nephew in town tomorrow morning, brand-new, and he can start practicing tomorrow afternoon."

Trixie looked at the tall groom and the slight figure beside him, and felt a glow of pleasure. It was good to see Regan feeling different about Dan. *He just didn't really know him,* she told herself. And then added honestly, *And neither did I, till tonight.*

Brian was standing beside her now, draping a blanket over her shoulders and forcing a cup of broth into her hand. "Drink every bit of it, and then we'll get on our way back to the horses. We left them at Mr. Maypenny's because there aren't any paths."

The broth tasted very good and chased away the chill. In a very few minutes, Trixie felt as good as new.

Brian brought the Thermos to offer her more, but she refused. "I feel great now. Let's start home. Moms must be simply frantic with worry about Bobby."

"She was frantic about both of you!" Brian said very soberly. "She was sure you had both been kidnaped by that tramp that robbed our clubhouse."

"The tramp!" Trixie suddenly remembered. "Dan!"

Dan looked surprised and put down his cup. The others looked questioningly at her, too.

"Dan!" she exclaimed again. "Tell them what that

awful Luke is planning to do! Maybc Regan can get there and stop him before he does it!"

"What's all this?" Regan demanded sharply, looking from Trixie to Dan.

Dan hesitated, scowling. Trixie snapped, "Go on! Don't forget what he promised to do to you because you wouldn't help him! It's not snitching to protect your own self from a person like him!"

So Dan, in a few words, explained Luke's intention of breaking into and robbing the Manor House.

When he had concluded, both he and Trixie were surprised to see that neither Regan nor Mr. Belden showed any alarm. Mr. Belden smiled, instead, and told him, "This Luke will run into big trouble if he tries it. Mr. Wheeler hired extra guards to patrol the Manor House grounds when he came home and found out the clubhouse had been burglarized. Luke will run head-on into them if he steps on the Wheeler estate."

"Whew! That's swell!" Trixie beamed. "Just think, Dan, if you had let him talk you into going there with him, you'd have been in trouble for sure!"

Dan nodded soberly, but he didn't have to say anything. They all knew how he must feel.

"Shall we get started for home?" Brian asked, to break the silence. And everyone began to bustle about, putting out the fire, gathering up empty Thermos bottles, and checking to see that they weren't leaving anything behind. They had no intention of coming back here again for a long, long time.

"And we're going to forget all about Bobby's lost shoe," Trixie's father told her when she suggested she might go into the cave and try to find it. "Mother will put away this one he's wearing, and he'll forget all about having lost a shoe here. We don't want him coming out to look for it!"

"And I'll see he's furnished with a kitten as soon as ever I can find one," Regan promised gravely. "We want no more expeditions like this one of his!"

"Oh," Trixie was reminded of the catamount. "Shouldn't we take along some burning torches," she asked nervously, "in case that wildcat is still around? He might jump down on one of us from a tree!"

Regan chuckled and patted the stock of his rifle. "His jumping days are over, Trixie. I got a good sight on him at less than twenty yards' range, and next time you see him, he'll be a rug for your room."

"I think I'll let somebody else have him," Trixie assured her grinning brothers. "I don't even want to think about that particular kitty again!"

Bobby lifted his head from his father's shoulder

and blinked around at them. "Where's the kitty? Can we go find the kitty now?"

Mr. Belden patted his shoulder and told him soothingly, "The kitty's run away, skipper. We'll have to find you another one."

Trixie, looking nervously around into the darkness, shivered. "And much smaller, please," she said, under her breath, "this time!"

And in a few minutes, they were all on their way trudging through the woods toward Mr. Maypenny's place.

Chapter 21
The Carnival

The old gamekeeper was delighted to see them all come trooping in, Mr. Belden carrying Bobby, and Mart and Brian lending a hand to their tired sister.

But he was surprised to see Dan Mangan trudging along at Bill Regan's side. "Where's the other?" he demanded suspiciously. "Where's the one that took you away?"

"He's in the hands of the law by now, Mr. Maypenny," Peter Belden told the old fellow.

"Good thing, too. And you're okay, Dan? I was afraid for you, after what he did to me!" Mr. Maypenny touched the sore spot on his head. "It still hurts."

"Everything's all right now, Mr. Maypenny." Trixie came up with a wide grin on her face. "And Dan's going to help us with the carnival, if you can spare him." She looked at him hopefully.

"Guess I can," he said drily. "Ain't seen much of him the last couple of days, and managed to get along somehow, just the same!"

"I'd be glad to stay and help all I can here," Dan told

Mr. Maypenny, "but Uncle Bill wants me to go back to the city with him for a day or so and sort of straighten things out with a man there."

"Humph! That judge, I suppose." He peered at Dan over his spectacles. "Well, I'll give him a letter to show that judge how much we'd like to have you stay on here, and I figure it won't take you too long to get your business finished with him."

"Thanks, Mr. Maypenny," Dan said with a grin. "I sure hope I can be back by Saturday."

"We're counting on it." Brian came up in time to add his voice.

A couple of minutes later, when Dan had walked over to their horses with Brian and Mart, Mr. Maypenny hurried over to Bill Regan.

"What's this about Dan having to go back to the city now? You're not thinking of letting them put him in that reform school, are you?"

Regan looked troubled. "When I went to the city this week, it was to tell the judge that Dan wasn't doing so well with the folks out here. Things looked pretty bad, you remember. So the judge said he'd issue papers and send the boy away to the school. I was supposed to turn him over tomorrow."

"Well, you can't do it now. Call the judge on the

phone and tell him it was all a mistake."

"I wish I could, but I'm afraid Dan'll have to go in with me. Maybe when I tell the judge what really happened out here, about this Luke fellow, who used to be head of the street gang, coming here and trying to make Dan help him rob the Wheelers—"

A small voice came from behind them. "It's all my fault everybody thought Dan was the thief," Trixie said unhappily. "I found some clues but they weren't true ones. And I'm awfully sorry."

"Forget it, Trixie. It wasn't your fault. Dan was pretty unfriendly to everybody when he came here. He gave a bad impression," Regan said honestly.

"If it would help, maybe Dad would take me to the city so I could tell the judge."

Regan smiled. "It won't be necessary, I hope, Trixie. I think when he's had a talk with Dan and I tell him the whole story, he'll let Dan come back with me. We'll soon find out."

But one day passed and then another, and still Regan didn't come back with Dan Mangan to tell them that everything would be all right.

"Just the same," Honey told Trixie as she sewed busily on a green and gold costume for Bobby to wear as the little leprechaun in the ice show, "I'm going right ahead with this. I *know* everything's going to be settled in time for Dan to get back."

Bobby had been delighted when they had told him what they were planning for him for Saturday. He had even stood still for a whole ten minutes while Honey tried on the half-finished costume. Regan had gilded Bobby's skate-shoes till they looked like solid gold, and Miss Trask had contributed a wonderfully golden feather for his peaked hat.

And Bobby himself had practiced solemnly on his figure eights and on his final bow. They didn't dare tell him that there was a chance his friend Dan might not get back.

The books were piled high in the storeroom at the farm, and practically every ticket had been sold. The prizes, from the toy bear to the secondhand lumber, were all on display in the local stores, waiting to be transported to the lake for distribution when they were won. The whole town was joining wholeheartedly in the benefit for the little school library in faraway Mexico.

Saturday morning came. There was still no word from Regan about Dan. Mr. Wheeler had told Regan to stay on in the city until the case was decided one way or the other, and the boys were doubling as assistant grooms, doing their own regular chores and getting last-minute tasks done before the carnival.

Honey came rushing into the clubhouse, the finished leprechaun costume over her arm. Her eyes were dancing. "The most wonderful surprise—" she began. But as Trixie looked up excitedly from pinning the clown costume on Mart, Honey clapped her hand over her mouth.

"Oh!"

"Ouch!" Mart yelled. "That pin went in an inch!"

But Trixie ignored him. "Is Dan back?" she demanded happily.

Honey shook her head. "Not that I know of. It's something else, but I promised not to tell you."

Mart groaned. "Here we go again! Hurry up and let me out of here so you can tell her!"

"I don't intend to! It's too elegant a secret to tell anybody. It would spoil it!"

Mart peeled off the almost-finished costume. "Can't hang around to hear it, but I bet it's a world-shaker!" And he grabbed up his jacket and marched out.

Honey giggled. "I know another secret, too. Mart's new jacket is almost finished. I nearly brought it along to show you just now. I didn't know he was here!"

"We'll give it to him after the show—an extra prize,

we'll tell him, for winning us the lumber for our floor here!" Trixie loved surprising people.

Honey danced around the room, throwing a lace mantilla around her shoulders and draping it over her head. "I adore my costume! Don't you love yours?"

Trixie nodded. "Only I feel sort of silly with my blond mop and a high comb tied on with a string so I'll look like a *señorita!*" She grimaced at herself in the mirror as she perched a tall comb on top of her head and it fell down on her nose. "Hope it doesn't blow right off my head when we're doing our fast spins!" She set it straight again and did a twirl.

In her dungarees, wool sweater, and sneakers, and with the comb tilting precariously over all, she made a funny picture, even to Honey, who was her most enthusiastic admirer. "Oh, Trixie, you're a card!" she giggled.

"If that's Spanish, I'll take vanilla!" a voice remarked from the doorway. Brian and Mart both had their heads stuck in, but as usual it was Mart who spoke. "Hey, did she spill that secret yet?" he went on.

"Indeed, I did not!" Honey laughed. "So don't come sneaking in hoping to hear anything. You'll all have to wait till tonight. That's final!"

Mart groaned. "Cruel wench! Just for that, we won't tell you who's down on the lake, practicing like mad!"

"Dan!" Trixie shouted. "Is it Dan, Brian?"

"None other, my sweet!" Brian laughed. "Regan cleared up the whole thing for him, thanks to Mr. Wheeler's letter and Mr. Maypenny's too. Dan's one of us."

"Hey, that's swell!" Trixie rejoiced.

"Too bad he couldn't be a Bob-White, but I guess he's too sophi—sophi—" Trixie had bogged down as usual, "whatever it is."

"Pretty close, toots," Mart told her with a grin. "The word is sophisticated, only it doesn't really fit Dan. I know he's panting to join us, even though he kidded our club when he first came to Sleepyside."

"Should we have a conference meeting and vote on inviting him?" Trixie asked eagerly. "This noon?"

"I've got two votes here," Mart pointed to himself and Brian, "and you two. And Jim will go along. That just leaves Di, and she always votes the way you two do. So why waste time conferring when we've got so much work to do getting ready for tonight at the lake?"

"Okay," said Madame President Trixie. "He's in! And we'll tell him tonight." She looked thoughtful suddenly. "Gleeps! Honey'll have to run up another jacket."

"Say, mine's too small anyhow. I can let him have it till Honey gets around to making me one that fits. Would you, will you, Honey?" Mart was sensitive about his wrists hanging out two inches from the jacket sleeves.

"Well," Honey winked aside at Trixie and pretended to look doubtful. "I suppose I could—some day."

But Mart still wanted Dan to have the jacket, even though he himself might have to get along without one for some time. "We can't have him seen around in that black leather jacket, once he joins the B.W.G.'s," he said soberly.

"Yes!" Trixie nodded. "It was his black leather jacket that set me against him from the first, and lots of other people might feel the same way, because so many tough characters wear them."

"Well, at least we know some guys in black leather jackets can turn out okay even if they've gotten off on the wrong foot," Mart admitted.

"And we know some others, like that Luke character, that don't have much chance of changing. And that reminds me, Mr. Lytell saw him at the Sleepyside jail when the guards from the Wheeler place brought him in, and he identified Luke as the one who sold him Honey's watch. So Dan didn't do that, after all, any more than he broke into this clubhouse."

"Well, it's all past now, and I'm glad," Honey smiled.

"Now how about that big secret?" Mart teased.

But Honey shook her head firmly. "Not till tonight!" And she stuck to that.

It was a beautiful night. Besides the moonlight that bathed the frozen lake in soft blue light, there were lanterns strung everywhere, and just enough breeze to keep them swinging gently.

Jim had rigged up a microphone, and when Dan recited the piece about the little leprechaun, and Bobby dashed around in his costume pretending to be that fairy shoemaker, the Sleepyside crowd applauded till their hands hurt.

Then it was Trixie and Honey's turn to glide about the ice, as twin *señoritas* from sunny Mexico, while a phonograph record attached to Jim's speaker system played *"La Paloma."*

And then the speed-skating competition began, and the boys from Sleepyside lined up against the boys from Round Point High.

Mart had been wearing his clown outfit all evening, acting as general funnyman and master-of-ceremonies. He wanted to get into the race most of all, because the prize was the flooring from the antique salt-box house.

"Gosh, hope I have time to change and get into the senior dash," he confided to Trixie, but the bunting on the souvenir booth had blown loose, and he had

to get a hammer and tacks and go to work on it.

He finished it just before the senior group lined up to race, and there was no time to change.

"All ready?" boomed Jim's voice.

And Mart made a mad dash to join the skaters. But the wide ruff around his neck blew up and got in front of his face before he ever got to the line-up. He didn't see the twig half-imbedded in the ice, and he went sprawling.

It was a hard fall that he took, and he lay there for a full minute, trying to shake his brain clear.

No one had noticed Mart's fall, and before he could scramble to his feet the starter's gun had barked and the race was on. He stood, dismayed, watching them speed past in a circuit of the lake, while the crowd cheered.

Around they went the second time, and now Mart heard Trixie's yell, "Dan!" and saw that Dan was well in the lead. He promptly forgot his own skinned knee and torn clown outfit as he joined his own voice to the yelling and shrieking.

And it was Dan who came in first!

And it was Dan who received the lumber company's order for the historic flooring. He promptly turned it over to Jim and Trixie, as the co-presidents of the Bob-Whites.

But the biggest excitement was yet to come. There

was a loud fanfare as the chatter and applause for Dan died down, and the hi-fi blared out the Mexican national anthem. A big searchlight that had stood draped in the background was run up quickly and turned onto two seats which had been unaccountably empty.

They were occupied now by two very scared, but very pretty, *señoritas,* dark-haired and big-eyed. They rose and bowed timidly as the public address system announced, in Jim's voice, that the special guests were the *Señoritas* Perez from San Isidro, Mexico, respectively Dolores and Lupe. It was for the benefit of their school library there that the carnival was being held, Jim announced, and now that the entertainment was almost over, the young ladies from Mexico would be glad to say hello to their friends.

It was a happy ending to a gay event as the boys and girls gathered around the *señoritas* to shake their hands and listen entranced to their shy conversation.

"So that was the secret!" Trixie exclaimed as she and Honey dashed over to join the crowd.

Honey nodded, her eyes starry. "They're staying at our house. Dad and Mother made their trip just special to surprise us by bringing the girls back. It took some managing, but Dad did it! And we've been invited to visit them in Mexico."

"Jeeps!" Trixie was overcome. "Mexico!" And she hugged Honey in delight.

But that was to come later. Right now everyone was getting out onto the ice to skate, and the smell of good food was being wafted over the ice, so Trixie and Honey hurried to join Lupe and Dolores.

They were a minute too late. Jim had Dolores and Brian had Lupe, on proud right arms, and the two couples were skating out onto the ice to join the rest of the happy crowd.

"Well, what do you know about that?" Trixie asked her best friend.

Honey giggled. "I know we won't be taking that trip to Mexico without our brothers, for one thing. And for another, I was just wondering if Lupe and Dolores have brothers at home who are as good-looking as they are themselves?"

"Probably not," Trixie grinned. "But I bet they'll be lots of fun! Let's go find Dan and Mart and do some skating ourselves!"

"All right, let's!"

But first they stopped a moment to open a package they had hidden inside the ticket booth.

And a few minutes later, as Trixie and Dan skated out onto the lake, closely followed by Mart and Honey, all four were wearing B.W.G. jackets, though Mart's was the only brand-new one. They looked very smart in them, except that Trixie still had on her Spanish comb and mantilla, because she hadn't been able to get the knot untied in the string that held the comb in place.

But she had a grand time in spite of it, and so did everyone at the ice festival, including Bobby, who had gone to sleep with his head on the toy bear, which was now his because the only other under-ten contestant had developed an early tummy-ache and had to go home before the race began.

And Regan, speaking for all of them at the end of the gay evening, told Mr. Maypenny, "It looked for a while as if the experiment was a mistake, but it seems to have turned out just fine."

To which Mr. Maypenny nodded and said, "Amen!"

Trixie Belden is back!

Don't miss any of her exciting adventures.

DI'S HALLOWEEN PARTY—
DI, TRIX, HONEY

BRIAN'S
JET-PROPELLED
BUGGY!

Bobby and friend

Bob-Whites of the Glen

THE CHAMP

SITZMARK JIM!